To Jeff

first name!

# SILENT CITY

G R Matthews

BFFF 2016
- 37/100

Copyright © 2016 G R MATTHEWS

All rights reserved.

ISBN: 153721473X
ISBN-13: 978-1537214733

# DEDICATION

For Su.

# CHAPTER ONE

"What the fuck are you still doing in this city?"

The question was heavy with the threat of violence. It wasn't a surprise. These things happened once, maybe twice, a month. The bruises had usually faded before the next set was inflicted. A fresh bottle of vodka was all I'd come out for. It was cheaper than whiskey and you could mix it with anything.

"I don't believe we have been introduced," I said, in the hope that I might be able to talk my way out of this. Judging by the snarl that rumbled up from the heavyset man's chest, maybe not.

"I don't like you," he said. Not an original line, but I suppose he felt he had to start somewhere. There were a couple of friends behind him, but they didn't seem to want to get involved. A small blessing.

"Really? You don't even know me." I backed up a step. "Perhaps if we sat down for a drink or two you might come round to liking me."

"I don't like you 'cos you killed them all." He took a step forward. I could see the veins and arteries in his neck pulsing. The problem was, I couldn't deny the accusation. I had killed them all.

"Listen," it was worth a try, "it went to court and all through the due process of law. Now all I want to do is go home, have a drink and get some sleep. Why don't you just walk that way and I'll go the other way. You'll never have to see me again."

I'm no ninety pound weakling and, like every person of my age and older, I'd done my service time. He must have had a couple of stone on me, if not more. Another step back and I looked around for assistance. Helpfully, my fellow shoppers had created a boxing ring out of their bodies to prevent my escape. The shopkeepers stood in their doorways, watching the spectacle. None of them made a move towards a communicator or city panel. Store camera's would catch the action from multiple angles and I'd bet this would be all over the clips later on. If I was lucky I might be able to see it through blackened eyes. Unlucky and I'd be seeing double or, even worse, not at all. I wasn't sure my medical insurance could cover the cost.

The big man took in the crowd, noting their unwillingness to let me pass, and grinned. He took a step forward and raised his thick-fingered hands up in front of his face, curling them slowly to form fists.

"I'm going to enjoy this," he said, moving towards me.

"I'm not." I switched the bottle to my right hand. There was no way I was getting through the crowd without fighting them all. It was a battle I was sure to lose. I sighed. "Come on then, get it over with."

He roared and charged. As his left foot stomped down, shifting his weight forward, he threw a right hook at my head. I stepped forward, into the swing, and down onto one knee. The sledgehammer of his hand passed over my head. The bottle in my hand, I swung upwards, between his legs, as hard as I could.

The great roar he'd given rose in pitch by several octaves into a high, squealing falsetto. I slid to the side as his hands lowered to grab his squashed balls. The squeal ended as he ran out breath and began to gulp in air like a goldfish.

I decided to do him a kindness he didn't deserve. Sometimes you have to help people who are in a lot of pain, it is the humane thing to do. However, no good deed goes unpunished and the bottle broke on the back of his head. The vodka splashed all over the floor, dribbling away between the metal grill. I was left holding the neck of the bottle.

"Fuck," I said, "and who roars before they throw a punch?"

His friends came out of the crowd, eyeing me warily. I

didn't move. They'd seen me take out their leader in the space of a few seconds. Mostly by luck, if I am honest. If he'd decided to grab rather than swing, I am not sure there is much I could have done. If I backed off now they'd just get a free shot at my back. I needed them to be scared of me.

"Pick him up and clear off," I said and took half a step forward, brandishing the sharp end of the broken bottle in their direction.

"You'd better watch out, mister," said one of them, a short, skinny fellow with nervous eyes. "He'll come after you."

"I know," I said. The crowd parted as I turned away from the fat man who rested face first in the puddle of my vodka. He'd get to drink more of it than me. The remnants of the bottle went into a recycling chute.

The police would be round later, the clips shows and the shopkeepers would inform them even if the crowd didn't. That's why I had made sure my vodka soaked friend had swung first. The cops knew me and I knew the law. At least those parts of it to do with getting accosted and beaten up.

I patted my pockets, looking for change and realised I couldn't afford another bottle.

"Bugger."

## CHAPTER TWO

I placed the two glasses down on my usual table at the back of the bar. It was early and most of the regulars hadn't shown up yet. Condensation trickled down the glasses and created one of those little rings of water on the table top. The smaller glass of whiskey was waiting for afterwards, my reward and sanctuary for the hard day's work.

Tom, the barman, had given me the usual spiel about it being 12 year old single malt. An obvious lie. One I am sure he kept up more by habit than any chance I would, one day, be so far gone as to believe him. There were no single malts anymore, hadn't been for a few hundred years. It was one of those inherited drinkers' memories that we all liked to indulge in. For some, it became the dream that someday they would find a fabled last bottle of Provenance or Glenfiddich.

The bar itself, one of many in the city, was right at the bottom end of the market. The glass tables were toughened to be pretty much unbreakable, the chairs bolted to the floor, there was a weapon scanner on the entrance, and I've seen the stun baton that Tom keeps behind the bar used a few times.

The clientele, the other drinkers like me, weren't a talkative bunch and that was fine. I didn't come here to talk. Sure, there was the occasional game to watch on the screens and we'd have a friendly bet or two to keep things interesting, but we were, by and large, a solitary bunch.

When the trading subs came in, the peace, quiet and solitude would be disturbed. Foreigners invading our carefully guarded personal spaces. The loud voices, raucous laughter and lewd jokes brought out the worst in our collective individualities. Tom liked the money coming in, but he shared our dislike or rather, I suppose, we shared his.

It's his bar after all. The barman sets the tone and the atmosphere. He didn't joke or try to engage us in worthless small talk, he served drinks and kept the place reasonably clean. He knew his place and role in our little deal – don't ask what you don't want to know, leave us alone and we will do the same for you, by the way, I'll have a whiskey and a beer to chase, here's the cash.

I came here for the quiet and the drink. Couldn't say I wanted the company, but staying in my tiny compartment watching clips every night wasn't any good for me either. Been three years now, same seat, same drink, same crowd. It took about six nights to find my seat. Everyone had their own and it was another of the unwritten rules of the place, you didn't hijack another drinker's spot.

The second rule of finding your spot was that of dead man's shoes. I'd got my seat in the dark corner because I'd heard one of the regulars, I don't know his name, come to think of it, I'm not sure of many names in here, say the previous occupant had died. I'd waited the night out on the table by the door and he hadn't shown. So, the next night, I got my drink and moved in. Nobody batted an eyelid.

It's the way things are. Once you understand the rules, you're in and accepted by the rest. I've watched a few newcomers find their own spot over the years, but I've watched many more struggle to get to grips with the place and never come back. Like whiskey, it's an acquired taste. You have to drink a full bottle to understand the appeal. Here, you just had to survive your first full month.

"Can I sit here?"

I put down my half-finished drink and looked up into her face. I didn't know who she was. Her eyes and smile seemed familiar. I'd seen her somewhere before, but for the life of me I couldn't think where.

"You've never been here before have you?" I asked.

"No, my first time." She sat gracefully, as if trained to.

Her long legs, emerging from the hem of an expensive business skirt, were hard to take my eyes off. She placed a drink, a small glass, mostly full, on the table. I gave it a quick look, but I'd no idea what it was. Over her shoulder, I saw Tom give a shrug of confusion. This lady wasn't playing by the rules and Tom seemed powerless. I could feel the eyes of the other patrons turn to look my table and didn't like the scrutiny. Taking a quick pull of my beer, I cracked the glass down harder than normal, making my point. The pressure of the gazes eased.

"Why here?" I asked, a little surprised at myself.

"Why not?" She removed her suit jacket and hung it from the back of the chair. "I knew this place existed and it seemed right to come here. Is there a problem?"

"No, no problem. Just curious. As you can see, we don't get many people like you in here?"

"Women?" She glanced around the bar, piercing the veils of isolation the regulars had spent years building up.

"Rich people." The bar was quiet. Not the usual quiet of drinking, but the deep silence of listening.

"I'm not rich. I just work for a rich man."

"Lady, you are richer than any of us." I gestured with my nearly empty beer glass. "This is our local. You're a long way from home."

"Do you want me to go?" Her eyes locked onto mine and I couldn't look away. There was a challenge in them, and recognition, but of what I couldn't say.

"No, that's fine. You're entitled to sit here. Just like the rest of us." Another one of those rules of the bar, you didn't kick anyone out. Plus, I didn't want her to go. There was some memory that I couldn't dredge up from the benthic of my mind. I knew it was there but it was too deep to find.

We didn't talk for a while. I finished my beer and picked up the imitation whiskey. It was always the smell of whiskey that I liked best, the earthiness of it. I'd been in arboretums and hydroponic bays, even worked in the algae vats that scrubbed the carbon dioxide from the air. They'd had a smell of mud, dirt and life. Whiskey had the same, just with a hefty kick of alcohol as an added bonus.

With both glasses empty, I needed another drink. I gave a quick glance to her glass, also empty. Now, I'd been raised to be polite, to be a gentleman around the ladies, but that upbringing was battling hard with the rules – you don't buy others a drink, unless you won the bet in a game.

Upbringing won. I stood slowly and tipped my beer glass towards her empty glass.

"Want another?" My voice was quiet, I hardly heard it myself, but she did.

"Sure and thanks." She smiled up at me, pristine white teeth without a kink or twist. She didn't belong here.

Tom watched me approach the bar, glasses in hand. He caught my eyes with his own and raised a questioning eyebrow. I had no response. Instead, I placed the glasses on the bar and indicated for the same again. I'd swear in front of a judge that Tom never took his eyes off me whilst he poured the refills.

"You want a snack with those drinks?" Tom asked as he placed the two full glasses on the bar. It was like he had thrown a bucket of deep water in my face. Another rule of the bar – you don't come here to eat, so don't ask.

"Funny, Tom," I mustered in response. "I hear there's a Polyneesey sub due in tomorrow."

The last trade sub from that part of the ocean had contained a below-par load of brewing ingredients which made beer tasting of rotten seaweed, we'd all suffered that month, and sailors that had made an absolute mess of the bar. To be fair to them, they'd paid for the damages but the damage to the beer had been almost too much to forgive. I could hear him muttering as I returned to the lady at my table.

"So," I began and then struggled to finish, "you go out looking for new bars much?"

I could have drowned myself in my drink right there and then. Listening back to the sentence in my own head, I was sure I'd just accused her of being an alcoholic, or worse, a bar-fly.

"Not really," her voice didn't contain any recognition of the insult. "I don't get out that much. When I do, I like to explore and see the sights of the city."

"The sights?"

"You know, the arboretum, the museum of the pre-flood times, the theatre, the library, the ruins of the first city. There is enough out there, if you know where to look. I've been to a lot of them for social functions, but to get time to actually look and take in the atmosphere of those places is wonderful."

"Sure." It was all I had and it was weak.

"Seriously." I could see she was warming to her subject and better that she did the talking than me. I hadn't got much to say. "The city is always changing. You have to stop occasionally to take it all in. The museum, for instance, all the stuff in there from the pre-flood has been salvaged from the sea floor. Some of the best bits are the photographs of the old world. Have you seen them?"

I shook my head.

"The colours, the trees, the buildings, and the sky. The sky is almost frightening. I remember my parents taking me out to one of the trenches not far from here. The Fe-products one, I think. That scared me, the ocean floor just dropping away into a darkness so absolute that it seemed to be swallowing me up. Above the water, in those photographs, there was the sky, blue skies, skies with clouds, sunlight seen through leaves, or between the buildings of their great cities. It seemed to carry on forever, a blue infinite world. I stared at them for a long time and couldn't stop thinking about the clouds and the sky. Why don't they fall on people? What's holding them up there?"

I was trying hard not to stare. There was passion in her voice, and longing. I hadn't heard either in years. She looked up from her drink and locked her gaze with mine, seeking something. I'm not sure she found it.

"You think I'm mad," she said and I think I probably did, "but I'm not. We've lived in this city, or the others, for centuries. Can you imagine something above your head so high that you'll never reach it or touch it? No ceiling to contain your world, no danger of drowning in the open spaces, no limit to your vision."

Now there she had a point. I couldn't imagine it. There have been stories, there are always stories, of sailors who'd gone to the surface. Either their sub had developed a fault and they'd needed to take on air, even the poisoned air of the world above, or they'd followed the old myths about riches on the islands that peeked through the waves. In the stories, they all went mad or died some horrible death. Probably just stories to frighten and keep us safe, but there were enough that some might have roots in the truth. If you dug down hard and far enough it would be there somewhere. It usually was.

I'd heard of a group, called themselves Skimmers, who would take their subs up near the surface and scuba just below the surface. The trick was, apparently, to get hold of some surface debris from the before, sell it on the antiques market and do it all without getting caught.

"The surface is dangerous." It was as statement of fact.

"Don't you want to live on the surface again?" she asked with a tilt of her head that I was beginning to find quite attractive.

"I never lived on the surface." I took a drink of my beer. "In fact, you'd probably have to go back to my great, great, grandparents to even remember someone who'd lived up there."

"I know that, but I like to dream. I'd like to believe that one day we can get away from this manufactured air, the constant hum of the machinery that keeps us alive and contained in this city."

"Well, you've come to the right bar to dream. We're all here trying to find our own way to cope with the pressures of life. Dreaming is as good a way as any of doing that, I suppose."

I couldn't help but feel a little of her longing for more

freedom. Life isn't like that. Only the rich could afford to dream, the rest of us had to work hard and forget.

"So, do you have a dream?"

"Every day I dream of a cold beer and whiskey to follow." It was a quick response and she probably thought me incredibly shallow. She was skirting a bit too close to me, the "me" I drank to hide from. That's why I came here. I watched a small smile flitter across her face at my response. Perhaps she thought it charming and witty or maybe she was just being polite. Whatever it was, it put a hold on the conversation for a while. We sat in silence sipping our drinks. The bar felt like it was returning to normal. All the regulars were relaxing back into their contemplative solitude with an inaudible but communal sigh.

"What did you say your name was?" Her question was polite and friendly, a way to get our conversation back on track, but chalk up another rule gone.

"Corin, Corin Hayes."

# CHAPTER THREE

I waited for the response.

When none came, I took a chance and looked up. She wasn't looking at me, her gaze was lost elsewhere. From the faint glow and flickers in her eyes, I could tell she'd been fitted. It might have been one of those permanent soft-wired in-eye systems or the temporary implants that bosses sometimes insisted their aides have. Either way, those little lights indicated she was accessing the city-web and that meant she was researching me.

Why bother? I mean, everyone in the city knew my story. It wasn't a secret. Hell, it had been the top news story for a month when it happened and I still got the occasional question from folks who had no concept of privacy. That's why I came here. The one bar in the city and now I'd have to face the questions.

"I should have remembered." Was not the response I expected, it was the one I got.

"Remembered?"

"Yes, I should have got it when I sat down. Been that kind of day, I suppose."

"What do you mean remembered?" Why I was even asking? My best bet was to be quiet, drink my drink, hope my name was enough to get a little sympathy and then get out of this situation as quickly as possible.

"I was there, in the court. It was part of my job." So that's where I had seen her before. Not well, but then the court had been full of people and most of it had been a confusing mess. Faces sped past, witnesses, journalists, clips presenters, lawyers, judges, the Mayor alongside the crowd of onlookers, do-gooders, nosey parkers and ghoul chasers. I couldn't tell you which one of those she was. I doubt that was one of the last bunch. She was too refined, too posh and that in-eye spoke of money and business. "I was so sorry about what happened. I had to transcribe the notes and summarise them all for the Mayor, that's who I work for."

"He sent a card, you know," I said.

"I know."

"Of course you do, sorry."

"The card was really from him, by the way. I arranged it, the Mayor asked me to. He made sure he signed it himself."

"You'll have to thank him for me." I tried to sound sincere, not angry. All I really wanted now was to forget. I hadn't had enough to drink yet and she was still here, in front of me, knowing it all, in detail.

"I will. He will be very glad you read the card." She sounded more sincere than I'd managed and I got the feeling it wasn't an act.

"Really?"

"Yes, really." The flickering light of her in-eye was gone and she had a far-away look back in her eyes. "The accident was the first real crisis he had to deal with when he took over. He felt, still feels, responsible. After all, it is his city to run and the buck stops with him."

"So it's selfish on his part then. He doesn't care about me or about..." I dragged in a big lungful of air. I wasn't ready to finish that sentence. "He just cares because he had to deal with the media and it looked bad because it happened on his watch."

She looked directly at me. It was a steady gaze. More than that, it was unrelenting. I could feel myself wilt under the pressure. I looked away.

"Let me get you another drink," and this time it wasn't me offering.

I sat there, in my guilt-upholstered chair, and watched her glide up to the bar to order the drinks. It shouldn't have been a shock, though it was, when Tom helped her bring them back to the table. We rarely got to see his legs. Most of us would have said he started at the waist and finished at the top of his bald head. How he moved behind the bar had remained an unexplored mystery, until now.

Now she had Tom breaking the rules. If you can't carry your own drinks, it's time you stopped drinking and went home. From the corner of my eye, I saw one of the long timers knock back his poison of choice and stagger out of the bar shaking his head. The world was changing.

"So," she started, "how is work these days?"

Perhaps she was letting me off the hook a little. "It's fine. I get enough jobs off the board to get by."

"And the other wet-welders?" Perhaps she wasn't. But she'd bought the drinks and it would be rude to throw them back in her face, metaphorically and physically.

"I don't talk to them much. They return the compliment." Which was certainly true. On a job, I never bothered to find out their names. They knew mine from the work docket and from the Fish-Suit. There weren't that many of us in the city and you could bet your liver and kidneys that there wasn't another one in the whole world taking their jobs off the board every day.

Only one percent of all Fish-Suit trainees lasted the course. For most, putting the suit on once was enough. I hated it as much as the next person but I could cope. Even in the early days, when everyone else was puking into the Oxyquid, the breathing liquid that swamped your throat and lungs inducing the instinctive fight against the fear of drowning, I wasn't going to be beaten. I don't have much self-respect, especially now, but I don't like being beaten.

"Sounds lonely." No kidding, I thought. "How do you cope?"

I moved my gaze slowly around the bar to indicate one answer to that question and added, "Born stubborn."

"I need to powder my nose," she said and rose from her seat. With a small smile she added, "Don't go anywhere, I'll be right back."

# CHAPTER FOUR

I sat back in the chair and rested my head on the wall. Now she had gone, I could let go of the cramp in my stomach and the ache in my shoulders. From my pocket I drew, carefully, a few folded pieces of card.

Opening the first, I stared, as I did every night, into the face of my child. Tyler had been fourteen when the photograph was taken, two weeks later was the funeral. I couldn't cope, not sure who could've. I'd thrown myself into work, and the bottle. The coroner's report, which revealed the sexual assault and the injuries inflicted afterwards, was more than my wife could take. She broke down. The city hospital worked hard, and I couldn't argue with her care, but she'd surrendered her hold on the world. The cops never caught the pervert and murderer. They'd even suspected me at the start. Another reason my wife had left us all.

Work, drink. Drink, work. That was my life back then. Not too different to now I suppose, but then lives had depended on me and I didn't care. The accident killed seven co-workers, my friends. That was the court case she was talking about. The judge had exonerated me of any guilt due to diminished responsibility. They took my licence and travel-docs off me. Two years later, I had the licence back and the psychs declared me safe. The travel-docs I never wanted back. I would be in this city, Tyler's city, until I died.

The picture was just a scrap really. Lots of Tyler's stuff had ended up ripped and torn. The anger and grief had done that. I just helped out by letting the drink give them free reign. Part of my treatment was to piece it back together and whilst I couldn't find it all, I did find bits. I gazed at the smiling face on the photograph and felt a sad smile form on my own.

"Your child?" she asked and reached out an open hand. I hadn't heard her return or know how long she had been watching me.

I swallowed and put the picture on her outstretched palm.

"A beautiful child. I am very sorry," she said in soft tones as she handed the photograph back.

"Yeah. Me too." It came out harsher than I'd intended. I wasn't going to apologise.

"Corin," she began, then faltered and had to regroup a little. "Corin, I don't want to tell you how to live. Ocean knows, I'm in no position to pass judgement, but once in a while it might be good to let someone in. Let someone care a little and take some of the burden off your shoulders."

"Lady, I did that a while ago. Look where it got me." Why she'd stuck with me through three rounds of drinks was a mystery. I'm not handsome, my charm is sorely lacking and my social graces were left in the gutter along with last night's dinner.

"And you think that is what either of them wanted?"

"They're dead and the dead don't want anything." I raised my eyes to hers and let a little bit of anger flare in them. I could see, in hers, only cool water though. Water always dampens a fire.

"Then, perhaps, the living can care and can want, for you. As soon as I recognised you, I sent a message to the Mayor. He's kept tabs on you through the city-web over the years. There aren't many with your skills and expertise, and, well, he wanted to make sure you were all right."

"Probably just wanted to make sure I didn't go insane and cause more damage." I finished the beer off in a few short gulps and wiped my mouth with my sleeve. "I don't want to be rude," I saw her eyebrows rise, "but I think it's time you left. Thanks for the drink."

"You're right, I think it is." She left her drink unfinished on the table. "Maybe, one day you'll let someone in and see it isn't all bad."

She stormed out of the bar. She'd never fit in if she couldn't follow the rules, never leave your drink unfinished.

## CHAPTER FIVE

I woke early and, as normal, I had a hangover. Not a bad one, only a three on my personal scale of one to ten. I'd never had a ten. The memory of the nine sent shudders down my spine.

Struggling out of the covers, I staggered the few steps into the shower and let the lukewarm water wash the night and the alcohol away. It worked for the former, but it had no effect on the latter. The painkiller took the edge off the headache and I sat at the small city-web access screen.

Tapping the keyboard, I brought up the job lists for today. There were one or two that suited me and I put in bids. The first was turned down straight away. A few moments later the second was accepted. At least I could earn something today. Next, I checked the news hub and apart from the usual reports of conflicts near the Antarctic oil fields there was nothing in the local area to worry or excite me.

The mail box was my last stop. In amongst the adverts for penis enlargements, hair regeneration creams and nights of passion with girls whose images promised paradise but were, probably, in reality, six foot four with arms like tree trunks and persuasive way of parting the unsuspecting sensation seeker from their money, was an invitation that looked genuine. The mail came from the rich girl last night. The one who worked for the Mayor. For some reason she, and he, wanted to meet. The meeting was set for tonight and in a restaurant that would consume all my earnings from today's job for just a glass of water with a slice of fruit in it. Ice would be extra. If they were paying, and the message hinted strongly that they were, I would go. It would make a change from the bar.

I closed the system down and headed out to work. I'm a

wet-welder. It's not glamorous. It is dangerous. It pays the bills. There aren't many of us around. The really good ones are usually on a permanent contract to the Company. The bad ones sell their skills on the job boards, just like I did this morning. The fact that I was reduced to working alongside the bad ones was, in part, my own fault. I'd been on contract once, but the court case put an end to that. It also meant that even on the boards I wasn't seen as a good risk.

Sure, some of the foremen who did the casual hiring knew how good I was and understood what had happened. They were few and far between. Even fewer when they had their own jobs to protect. If something went wrong when I was on shift, it would be their neck on the line.

I managed to find enough work to get by and my rep was slowly building. In another ten years or so, it might be high enough and people's memories fuzzy enough that I could try for another contract.

The skin-tight under-layer of the Fish-Suit was always a struggle to pull on. A cloud of talcum powder and swear words accompanied the activity. The exoskeleton which encased my whole body, protecting me from the hideous pressure at this depth whilst being flexible enough to do delicate work, was easier. Out of the water, it was bloody heavy and moving was real chore, but it was only a few meters to the airlock and the suit charging station it housed.

The outer doors closed and I attached the cables to the connectors on the suit. The red hose charged the power systems and I watched the suit run through its pre-launch checks on the heads-up display. All systems showed green. The next bit was the worst, and also the reason why there were so few of us. I gave the command, pressing the finger controls inside my glove. If I'd been in a full pressure personal sub, a worker sub, I could have used voice commands. In a Fish-Suit, you can't speak.

The lights on the blue hose came on and I could hear the whistle of air being sucked out of my suit. It became harder to breathe. Thick gel entered the suit and started to pool around my feet and legs. It rose past my knees, hips and belly as I struggled to draw enough air into my lungs. It was always this way. You couldn't help but feel the fear as you ran out of air.

I fought the natural instinct to panic and rip the suit off. The gel rose past my chest and over my chin, mouth and nose. I held my breath, we all did at this point. We knew what was happening, but there is an inbuilt reflex no one could overcome. There wasn't a Fish-Suit user who couldn't chill your spine with the story of their first time.

The last of the air escaped my lungs in one sharp, bubble filled, burst and I gagged mightily as I sucked in the gel. Some users, at this point, are sick and have to go out with the chunks swimming around their visor. One or two, so the stories go, had choked and died on their own vomit.

The gel filled my lungs and though it felt like drowning, I didn't. It was this that put most folks off. The alternate feelings of suffocating, then drowning were not something everyone wanted to go through day in, day out. Some trainees said once was enough and gone back to the worker subs and other professions.

Anyway, this wasn't my first time. I lost count years ago. The gel was full of oxygen and although my chest ached to push the gel out and drag more in, I knew it wouldn't kill me.

The visor indicated the last of the checks complete and water poured into the cubicle. Once the room was full, I tapped out the instructions to open the outer door and used the thrusters, small but powerful water jets, to move out into the open ocean.

City lights gave the water a green glow. Other lights, embedded in, or tethered to, the sea floor increased the visibility to about fifty metres. Not too bad at this depth.

The sea is never quiet. There is always noise. Close to the city, the deep hum of the generators and the clanking of people and machines churning out whatever it was they made. Further away it became quieter, but the sea is a good conductor of sound. I've heard many things over the years, the deep thrum of whales shouting to each other over the miles, the moan of the sea floor moving, rhythmic thumps of, well, whatever it was that thumped rhythmically out there.

My visor showed the location of today's work site, not too far away. Using the thrusters, I turned myself around and got moving. Fish-Suits were never quick. There wasn't the room, or need, for a large battery to drive faster thrusters.

The job wasn't likely to take long. The suit could keep me in the water for almost a day if I needed it too. I'd done that once. It wasn't something I wanted to repeat. On the visor scanner, I could see two full-suits which would do any heavy lifting, and a mini-sub that contained the foreman. As I approached, I logged into the work-web to see the current state of play and to get my instructions. Simple support welding and water seal work. Boring. No challenge.

A few hours later it was done. I watched the payment enter my bank account in a little window on the HUD and headed back to the airlock to de-suit and get some food. The worst bit about the de-suiting? Getting the gel out of your lungs.

It burned like fire on the way up, your ribs ached as you pushed as much out as possible in one big heave. Then there was the coughing as your lungs tried to expel every last bit. All the time your own reflexes and reactions were trying to drag in as much air as possible. There'd been a time or two, maybe more, that in between a cough and gasp, I'd cover the floor with my breakfast, or lunch depending on the time of day. It wasn't unheard of and I'd stopped being worried about it years ago.

## CHAPTER SIX

I got to the restaurant early. It hadn't been hard to find the right clothes to wear. A single white shirt and pair of trousers were the only smart clothes I owned. I'd had a suit once, just for the court appearances. Once the court case was over, I shoved it down a waste chute.

The maître de gave me the dismissive once over. The look on his face when I gave him my name and he found it on the reservation list was worth the insulting looks. I'm damn sure he enjoyed the petty revenge of giving me the spare tie to wear. Yellow is not my colour.

He walked me to the table, past the other diners who obviously shared his disdain. A waiter was there, waiting, with the wine list. A quick flit around the city-web earlier to see what current dinner trends were suggested the new craze was to resurrect old languages and stick them on menus. If you were rich, you were educated. More importantly, if you were rich you had the implants that would translate the menu for you. I ordered a beer and put the wine list on the table without opening it.

She arrived, with the night's bill payer, when I was halfway through my beer. I stood up to greet her, them. I'd been raised to be a gentleman. It had slipped a lot over the years, at times I'd forgotten completely, but it was still there, when I needed it.

"Corin," she said by way of a greeting whilst I desperately fought to roll my tongue back into my gaping mouth, "let me introduce you to Merrick Storn, Mayor of the City."

"Corin, good to meet you." The Mayor put out his hand to be shaken and I had to focus to grasp it on the first go. The hand shake was firm and I was strangely glad he didn't do the politician's second hand over the first and pat routine. There was a knowing look in his eye as he said, "I know, but I didn't employ Derva just for her looks. She is an incredible organiser and keeps me on track every day. I couldn't be without her and she knows it."

"Please, sit," he continued and moved smoothly round the table to hold the chair for Derva, beating me to it. She folded her slim frame, coated in a deep red dress, into the waiting chair and gave her boss a small smile.

The waiter re-appeared and handed out the menus. I had no idea what they said. The websites had been right. For all I knew, I was holding the bloody thing upside down. A glance at Derva and the Mayor told me they were either better actors than I was or could read the menu without any trouble. Derva, I knew, had the in-eye and by the extension of simple logic the Mayor would have them too.

"A lot to choose from." It was a weak cover. Derva looked up from her menu to favour me with a smile. I'd dissect that one for meaning later.

"I've eaten here a time or two recently," the Mayor said. "Would anyone be offended if I ordered for us all? There are some excellent dishes on the menu and," at this point he leaned in and lowered his voice, "if you're not too bothered, we can share them around. There are some I would like to try and the chef here changes the menu quite often."

I waited for Derva to speak first, it was only polite. When she agreed so did I and the sweat of fear that had begun on my lower back evaporated. It was a safe bet to say that the Mayor was quite aware of my troubles and had just bailed me out. My cynical side was telling me he had it all planned, a consummate politician. I didn't care. He'd saved me from being embarrassed in front of a pretty girl and that was fine with me.

The Mayor beckoned the waiter over and placed the order. Just to show off, I'm sure, he ordered in the language of the menu. The waiter repeated it back and the mayor corrected the mistakes in pronunciation.

"Does irritate me, this fashion for resurrecting dead

languages," the Mayor said. "And they don't even teach their waiters to speak it properly. Pointless."

"Well, I didn't get a word of what either of you said, but if it tastes all right then I won't mind," I replied.

"The future is where it is at, Mr. Hayes. The past is there to be looked at and mulled over. We don't need to resurrect it. Look where the past got us." He indicated the walls of the restaurant. "We live in the deep sea, surrounded pressure that could kill us in an instant, with no access to the surface world that is our natural home."

## CHAPTER SEVEN

When the food arrived, I tucked in. I rarely get to eat so well. A diet of processed and flavoured algae impregnated with proteins and vitamins is my normal fare. The occasional piece of fish or seafood was a treat and only after a good week of work. Overfishing in the early years led depleted stocks that had yet to recover, fresh fish is expensive. The algae was cheap and easy to produce, a by-product of the carbon dioxide scrubbing that had to be done to keep our air breathable.

Over dinner we made small talk and the wine flowed sweet. Derva was making strong inroads into the alcohol, without any seeming effects. I'd put the Mayor in second place and me last. I was taking it carefully, that cynical voice was still there. The one part of the menu I had been able to make sense of, the numbers, had scared me more than the language barrier.

After the main course, an absolutely delicious mix of fish pieces and lobster in some sort of spicy sauce, I leaned back in my chair and struggled not to undo the top button on my trousers.

"Not too bad, wouldn't you agree?" The Mayor placed his knife and fork down on the silver edged plate in front of him.

"Very tasty. I don't think I have eaten so well in, well, ever." I replied. "But, I don't think you invited me to dinner just to show me a good meal. If you did, thanks."

"I'm glad you enjoyed it." He took a sip of his white wine. "It was Derva's idea. She spoke to me this morning of her meeting with you last night and reminded me of past events. I recalled your court case with sadness, though it was overshadowed by your daughter's accident three months before."

He paused for another sip of wine and I tried hard to keep the lump out my throat.

"I'd only been Mayor for month when they found her. You have my deepest sympathies for your loss. It means nothing to you, I know, but that day was one of the worst of my whole career. Then the court case, you had no luck there at all."

"Would you get to the point, please?" Re-hashing my past was not something I wanted to do. The bar existed so that I could avoid this very thing. I wanted to be polite though. For a start, this was the Mayor, the man in ultimate charge of all our lives, and he was paying for the meal. Until he did, I couldn't be sure I was getting out of here the rent money still in my account.

"Sorry. Very upsetting to dwell on the past." Another sip of wine. "Derva had me thinking and I did a quick bit of digging into your file. Very impressive references and work record up until that, well, you know. Anyway, it occurred to me that a man with your skills, the Fish-Suit licence and experience of working at all depths could be quite useful to the Corporation. I spoke with Head Office about a contract position in the company. A trouble shooter, someone who could drop everything and head off on jobs, get them done with a minimum of fuss and without all the bureaucracy that normally surrounds this kind of work. It didn't take long for them to agree with me."

"This is a job offer?" I needed a drink now and something a lot stronger than the wine I'd had with my main course.

"Of a sort. You won't have work every day, or even every week, but we will pay you a retainer and expect you to be ready to go wherever and whenever we say. In-between, you're free to work on short term jobs. Don't take on any long term projects. You never know when the company will need you."

"The Mayor has spent most of the day negotiating and clarifying this job offer. I know it must seem strange,"

Derva paused for a sip of wine, "but he was, and is, very sympathetic to the situation you find yourself in. The accident your boy suffered and the court case can't be fixed, but he can do something to make life easier."

"Very nice of him," and I turned from those dark eyes to the Mayor, "of you. There are lot of folks in need, why me?"

"Corin, why not you?" The Mayor finished his wine, poured another glass for himself then topped up Derva's and mine. "That's what you need to ask yourself. Sometimes it is better not to question things too much and accept what is being said to you, face to face. I really do feel sorry for your situation and I'm doing something to help you out. Are you in the position to turn it down?"

He had a point. Hell, many good points and all of them made sense, especially the one about money, the retainer. The only thing I found annoying, the continued use of the word accident to describe what had happened to Tyler. I took a slow drink from my own glass, thinking.

"How much of a retainer?"

It was Derva, not the Mayor who answered that one. She passed me an envelope which I duly opened and read the figure inside.

"When can I start?" I smiled at them both.

"Come to my office tomorrow and we can sign the contracts." The Mayor gave me an open smile and raised his glass. "Let's toast our new employee, Derva."

## CHAPTER EIGHT

Three weeks into the contract and life was good. Even better, I hadn't had to do a thing for it. I still did the daily contracts and checked the job board every day. Working was better than sitting around my tiny little apartment all on my own. I hadn't seen Derva since the signing, but the tortoise always beats the hare. Least it did in the story that I used to tell Tyler.

Breakfast was, as ever, an uninspiring affair. The excitement was the message from Derva in my mail box. Fair enough it was to a meeting in the Mayor's office at 10am. The tortoise was still in the race.

I turned up on time and wearing a tie. This time I'd gone for a colour that suited me. Black goes with everything. Creating a good impression was the right thing to do on your first day at work.

The Mayor's office was at the top of the city's central dome. These were the oldest parts of the city and the place where the rents were highest. They were a status symbol for the rich and idle. The workers, like me, lived in the boxes, the cheap additions that the company had bolted on to cope with rising populations. They were hastily put together and took a good deal of looking after. I should know. I'd built a few in my time. Once they'd been stable for a decade or two they weren't too bad.

The domes though, they were different. Many were built in the years before the human race was forced to abandon the surface, and built properly. They were dual hulled and transparent. You could see the ocean above the dome which gave the illusion of space and freedom. People paid a lot for their illusions. Dominating the skyline was the central building that rose all the way to the inner hull. The corporation hadn't been so garish as to place their name in mile high letters down the building, but you knew who it belonged to. It made that kind of statement.

### # # #

I rode the elevator to the top floor, the old world classical music was supposed to induce a feeling of calm. By the eightieth floor it was irritating. The doors opened with a melodic chime, some sort of safety feature no doubt, and I was met by Derva.

In her work clothes she was still stunningly attractive, but now the added authority of business dress conjured all sorts of thoughts and visions.

"Derva, it is good to see you. To be honest, I thought I'd be met by a foreman or somesuch who'd give me the bare bones of the job. When your receptionist told me to come to the top floor, the Mayor's office, I was a little surprised."

"Corin, I hope you had a good breakfast and a pleasant journey here. I understand there was some congestion between your apartment complex and the central dome." The standard business response wasn't what I'd been expecting. I suppose she was on the clock and a certain level of decorum was expected. "The Mayor will brief you on the job in a few minutes. He is just finishing a meeting. Can I get you a drink?"

"Coffee would be good. Thanks. No whitener or sugar." I watched her walk to the drinks station in the corner of the room. I would have liked to watch her walk back, but that would be a little too obvious.

I sat in one of the leather chairs. Probably real leather too, from one of the vat-farms. Bloody expensive stuff. All my furniture was standard plastic, even the bed. The illusion of comfort came from a thin foam mattress and alcohol.

The coffee tasted dark and bitter. It was one of the few non-alcoholic drinks I enjoyed. There were some of those corporation magazines on the low table and I flicked through them while I waited. Every article focused on some new venture, a successful product, or up and coming member of staff. If you read them all, cover to cover, I don't reckon you'd actually learn much of how the world worked, but you'd be damn sure that the Corporation should be the centre of your existence.

"The Mayor is free, please follow me." Derva came round from behind her desk and waved me through the frosted glass double doors into a large room.

The Mayor rose from his comfortable seat and walked over to confidently shake my hand. "Good to see you again. Can I get you a drink?"

"Water would be good." Two coffees and I'd start getting twitchy.

"Have a seat, make yourself comfortable, and we'll get the briefing started." The Mayor indicated one of the low blue arms chairs. There was no desk in the room. Instead it seemed to be divided up into different areas. The comfy area, the table and chaired meeting area, the small round table supported by a single metal pole was probably the quick meeting area. Every different bit seemed to have its purpose and the comfy area was, I guessed, the briefing area.

I sank into the most comfortable chair I have ever sat in. As soon as my buttocks touched the fabric, it started to mould itself around me. The back support cushioned and supported at the same time. It was so good that I didn't even need to do my customary bum shuffle to find the right spot. The whole chair was the right spot. Next to me, a slender column of clear plastic rose from the floor. My glass of water sat on top, with ice cubes delicately chinking and a slice of lime floating between them.

"Well Mr. Hayes, the day has finally come. We have your first job, and your travel papers." The mayor smiled as he spoke. "Sorry it has taken so long. We had a few minor, technical difficulties getting your papers released, but they were quickly ironed out. Bureaucracy is ever the enemy of progress."

The smile said more than the words. The bureaucracy was likely some corporation lawyer disagreeing with his choice. There is no law in the cities except that which the corporations pay for, and impose. If they can pay for it, they can break it, and they did. The idea of a fair society had drowned a long time ago. It said a lot that he had been willing to argue my case and I picked up my water, dipping it towards him in a small gesture of acknowledgment.

"What is the job?" I asked.

"One of our small factory cities near the ridge has reported some stress fractures in its supporting struts and superstructure. Nothing major yet, but they need the struts micro-scanned to determine the pattern and cause," the mayor said.

The ridge meant the one down the middle of the Atlantic Ocean and, really, ridge was a misnomer. It was a long line, almost ten thousand kilometres, of constantly erupting volcanic mountains and fissures. New land being created in the centre pushed the land either side further apart. The thing is, all that new land is full of minerals and metals ripe for exploitation. With all that land moving, even slowly, the ground under the cities footings was moving too.

"A pretty standard check then?" I said and couldn't really see what they needed me for. A single-man sub with the right attachment could do the job. So I asked.

"This particular city is situated in an area with especially uneven topography. I am given to understand that the footings cannot be accessed by a small sub and that the lack of dexterity in the robot arms is a factor too."

I grunted. It made a certain amount of sense. Fish-Suits could work in areas that no one else could reach, or do jobs that needed a high degree of exceedingly careful work. However, there was something I wasn't being told. A little bump of suspicion began to itch between my shoulder blades.

"Which city?" I asked.

"Calhoun." There was a little flicker of the muscles around his eyes as he said it.

"Never heard of it." Which meant it had to be a tiny

place or, and this was my main concern, it was a Silent City.
"Where is it?"

There was that flicker again. Guilt or accessing files? The bloody implants had made reading people's eyes and emotions much more difficult. Poker was dead game these days. "It is in the Faraday fracture zone."

I don't have any in-eyes. I have to rely on the old standby of memory. I could picture a map of the ocean, quite detailed close to this, my home city, and becoming increasingly vague the further away I tried to recall. The Faraday zone was in the far north of the corporation's zone of influence. Every corporation, big or small, had a zone. Sometimes they were agreed by treaty and mutual consent. Sometimes they were fought over, constantly.

NOAH, the corporation that owned this city, claimed much of the middle and north Atlantic, from the coast of old North America all the way to the landmass of Europe. The northern border, if you could call the overlapping and fluctuating zones something as permanent as a border, butted up against the zone claimed by VYKN. They claimed all the land under the ice sheets of the North Pole. The Faraday zone was, and this filled me with joy, in that overlapping territory.

"The Faraday zone? Isn't that in a contested area?" I asked.

"Not currently," he answered. "VYKN have claimed the area, as have we, but we are working with them on a project to exploit the geothermal energy in the area. You'll need to stopover on the way and transfer to company sub that will take you directly to Calhoun."

"When do I leave?" I had my doubts, but I'd been getting paid not to work and it had felt strange. Now I would have to do something to actually earn the money I'd been spending. Switching to company sub meant that either factory town was brand new and no transport company had set up a route yet, or it was the thing I feared, a Silent City.

"There is a passenger sub leaving tomorrow morning,"

he said. "Your suit will go into the cargo hold."

"I'll be on it." I drank the rest of water. "Can you forward the city plans to me?"

"The plans will be on the company sub. You will have time on board to do all the planning you need."

Plans that can't be forwarded to a company device, secured by their own protocols and web teams, confirmed my fears. I was going to work in a Silent City.

## CHAPTER NINE

In my little compartment, I started packing. Into a small bag I shoved some underwear, a couple of t-shirts, my Fish-Suit undergarments (a smooth, skin tight all-in-one), and a toothbrush. I didn't own much. There was one other item I needed and I'd have to go out and buy it.

I left the bag by the door on the way out. The corridor was dark. They always are this far down in the city. Small electric bulbs provided a meagre illumination. Enough to make your way from one to the next in comparable safety, not enough to make out any details.

The metal grill floor gave a little under my weight, a sure sign that it was old and in need of some maintenance. The latter was unlikely to occur until there was an accident and only then if someone kicked up enough of a stink.

At the end of the corridor I turned left, then right and left once more to reach the section bulkhead. The door was open. It was always open. The city's emergency services controlled the doors. They only closed during an emergency and they wouldn't open till it had passed or everyone was dead. A hull breach, in any part of the city, would trigger these doors to close. There was no manual override. The wheel lock was provided to reassure people. Give them an illusion of control.

I'd known cities use the bulkhead doors to contain riots, to capture escaped felons or, in some extreme cases during conflicts, to sacrifice part of its population to save the rest. Some cities, those in the ISIS and DHATU corporations especially, had used the doors to solve a religious crisis or two. At least, that's what I heard.

Past the bulkhead door, stepping over the raised section into which the door slid, and I started up the stairs. No lifts for those of us at the bottom. I'd been known to stumble down every flight of stairs after a night in the bar. I'd also been known to struggle to reach the top the morning after. This evening it wasn't too bad and I was only slightly out of breath when I finally staggered out onto the lowest floor of the secondary dome.

These lower floors were a little better lit than the maze of corridors and levels that made up the living cubes. Up another level and I was amongst the cheap shops, stalls, bars and little workshops that folks ran to scrape a living in the city. I tended to do most of my shopping here.

I had a quick look around, just to make sure there was an absence of "friends" or other people who'd quite like to meet me in a dark secluded place and make their feelings known. This evening the coast seemed clear. Without any further delay, I made my way to the shop I wanted and, with a final quick peek over my shoulder, entered.

"Corin," the shopkeeper called.

This was a tiny shop selling specialist goods, if you knew how to ask. The door in was also the door out and a counter, with the shopkeeper behind, lined the back wall. Behind that was the only other door which led, I guessed, to the storeroom.

"Hal," I replied.

"You're back sooner than I expected." Hal leaned forward on the counter, resting on his elbows and crossing his arms.

"Going away for a bit," I said. "Knew I'd be missing your special brew if I didn't take some with me."

"Where you off to? Didn't think you could travel anywhere?"

I placed one hand on the counter. "Got my travel papers back and a job. That's where I am going, to do the job."

"Things are finally on the up then?" Hal clapped once, in celebration, I think. It could have been disappointment, he was going to lose his best customer for an unspecified amount of time.

"Seems so. So, you have any?" I asked.

"One bottle, I think. From the last batch. I wasn't going to start a new brew for a few days. Have to space them out or the waste sensors pick up on the chemicals."

"How much?" I asked.

He named the price and I winced. "That's twice the last bottle."

"This is the last bottle," he replied. "You have a job, you can afford the price."

"I haven't been paid yet," I tried.

"Shame, but that's the price." He was giving me a measuring look. I tried to paint my face with innocence, need and the determination to leave without it. He must have seen something of that as he said, "Ok, tell you what. You pay that price now and I'll give you discount on the next bottle."

I paused. This was the last bottle. I couldn't get it anywhere else. Certainly, if I was going to a Silent City, the chances of finding a dealer were slim to none. With none being the bookies favourite.

"Fine." I handed over the cash.

He ducked out the back and returned with a small neatly wrapped package. "Good batch this."

"Yeah," I agreed. I slipped the package into my pocket. It wasn't heavy. A single drop of this could make you forget the last few years if you weren't used to it. I was. "I'll see you when I get back and I won't forget about the discount."

I stepped out of the shop and into trouble. To be truthful, I stepped into and then bounced off the source of trouble, a thickset, pot-bellied man with arms made of muscle.

"Sorry," I said without looking up. A quick apology can often take the heat out of any situation.

"Well, well, well," he said and the bottom fell out of my stomach which, even considering it could have been the opposite way round, was not a nice feeling. "I've been wanting to bump into you."

I took a step back. "You have?"

"Yes, indeed. I surely have."

His face, those piggy eyes and the snarl on his lips sparked a memory. Not that I could place him, but I knew the face from somewhere. "How can I help you?"

"By standing very still whilst I knock your teeth out," he said and I noticed something I really should have seen before. He wasn't alone. There were three friends with him. None of them as big, but all of them smiling. He gestured to them and they spread out, encircling me.

"Are you sure you've got the right person?" I let my hands fall to my sides and checked the door I'd just come through. Hal beat me to it and slammed it shut. I heard the locks click, loud in the violent silence.

"I remember you from the accident, the trial and the time you crushed my knackers with a bottle of vodka." The big man grinned, crooked teeth and bad gums. "And now you're going to remember me."

"Fuck," was the only word I said. This was going to be painful, no doubt. All I could hope was that they'd miss the package if they decided to rob me afterwards.

They'd moved into a basic cross pattern. Me in the centre, the big guy straight ahead, one to either side and one behind. The corridor was clear too. Everyone seemed to have found just the shop they were looking for and dived in to make a purchase. There were cameras here. I doubt they were checked regularly and only if someone reported a crime. Not many down here reported a crime because any investigation would turn up some things they'd rather keep hidden.

"You sure about this?" I said, just to make sure there was no way out. The big guy grinned again, punctuating it by pounding a fist into his palm.

I scanned the environment looking for anything that might be weapon, or made into one. True to form, there was nothing. This was going to hurt. Four on one was bad news for the one. I lifted my hands, as if to surrender, to give up, and saw the ugly man's grin widen. The rest of his crew settled back onto their heels. They imagined, I hoped, that it was already over and were looking forward to a little entertainment.

As soon as that tension relaxed I moved, stepping backwards and striking with my elbow. The shock of the impact ran straight up arm into my shoulder and down through my hips. It felt solid to me, but nothing compared to how the victim felt. The clatter behind suggested he had dropped to the ground. I ignored this small victory as the two to the side started moving forward.

My great haymaker never reached its target. The guy to the right caught my arm at the elbow. The target, the left hand man, grabbed my other arm and cinched it tight against his body, pulling me off balance. I was caught.

The big man stepped towards me and, if anything, his smile was even wider than before.

"I am going to enjoy this," he said and swung his meaty fist, hard towards my face.

I did what I could. Kept steady between the two men, there was no way to dodge the fist so I rolled my head away, and hoped the blow would glance off.

# PART TWO
# CHAPTER TEN

The first leg of my journey would take me to a NOAH military city, just the other side of the Laurentian channel near Newfoundland. Past that and the ocean was contested territory. NOAH and VIKYN would operate patrols, but it was an area where a brave man could make his fortune or lose his life. The journey there would take about two days, give or take an hour or two. The passenger sub could make forty knots at a push and the captain, in his welcome and safety speech, reckoned we'd be doing a steady thirty-five all the way.

That was fine with me. The passing of time would let the painkillers work their magic and the company provided derma-patches to heal the worst of my injuries. I could recall the early hours of the morning, when I didn't want to open my eyes. The pain in my skull, jaw and stomach all rated high nines. My hands had been tied to the bed and looking around, trying to make sense of the ghostly, blurred images, it was apparent I was in hospital. Judging by the large blue blur near the slightly larger silver-white blur, that I took to be the door, I was under guard. A white blur had entered and stabbed something into my neck and the blurs darkened.

When I woke next, Derva was sat next to the bed, her bag in her hands. I noted the way she gripped it, white knuckles and fingers. She was stressed. Next to her stood a doctor.

"You've been beaten quite badly," the doctor had said as if it was news to me. "Luckily we have reset the two broken ribs, they'll ache for a few days, and your arm. That will ache too. You were lucky not to get a broken jaw. We had to reseat a few of your teeth. Try not to eat any tough food for a while. Soup would be a good choice. We put your nose back into place. The best we could at any rate. It looks as though it has been broken a few times and reset badly once or twice along the way. Other than that you have some cuts and bruises that the derma-patches will sort out in a day or two. They'll also take the edge of the pain as your bones knit themselves together – we've accelerated that as much as we dare. Make sure you eat lots of food over the next few days. You'll feel tired."

"You mean eat a lot of soup," I said.

"Anything soft that you don't have to chew too much." The doctor had no sense of humour I could detect. "Other than that, we have done everything we can and you'll be released in an hour or two."

The doctor had turned on her heel and left without another word. Derva stared at me for a few minutes. I tried to smile back at her, but my head hurt too much to keep it up.

"Who did this?" she asked.

"No idea," I answered. The frown on her face said she didn't believe me.

"Why did they do it?"

"You've seen my record. I get hit every so often. Lot of folks lost their lives in the accident and lot of those had a lot of friends. I am not popular."

"Was it over," and she leaned forward to whisper the next words, "drugs?"

"What? No, of course not." The small package? Had someone found it? It depended who had brought me in. The police and they'd have searched me first. A medical team and they'd have called the police, who would have searched my belongings as they were stripped off me. That might explain the guard at the door.

It was remarkably bizarre and surreal moment when she dipped her hand into her bag and brought out the package. I looked at it, at her, back to it and, finally, back to her.

"Is that mine?"

"You had it in your coat pocket when they brought you in." She didn't say anything else.

"Can I have it back then?"

"Why do you need this stuff? You know it is illegal. You could end up on a garbage sub for the rest of your life if you're found it with."

And she had a point. Anyone who got assigned to a refuse sub spent the rest of their very short life there. Well, to be truthful, they spent the bit of life they had left shovelling the garbage and then eternity as part of it.

"A shop near where you were found was raided last night and an illegal lab was found. The shop keeper is in custody and investigations are under way."

I held my breath, waiting for the next bit of bad news. I'd been caught with an illegal narcotic, near a lab, and been beaten up in the process. The only thing left for her to say was that the court had sat in my absence, that happened a lot to poor folks down here, and that I was garbage sub bound.

"You're lucky I have a city-web net out there. Any mention of your name in the system gets flagged up to me. I was here before the police."

And I could breathe a little again. "Thanks."

"I am going to keep this until you get back," she stood, "and then we will talk. The police are outside. They want to get your story and I suggest you make it a nice simple one. The sub is leaving on schedule. Be on it."

"Thanks," I said again.

"We will talk." And all the stress in that sentence was on the word in the middle.

After the police interview, I'd rushed back home, grabbed my bag and ran as fast I could, the doctor was right about the ribs, to the sub dock. I was settled in my assigned seat just as it pulled away from the docks.

Now, I just had to sit here. Sleep when I could. Drink when I couldn't - if they'd let me - and try not to think too much.

### # # #

Hours, and several sub-standard travel meals, later I arrived at the military city. Imaginatively, they called it Base 1. It was the third one built, and that tells you all you need to know about the military thinker.

The sub docked and I shuffled off alongside everyone else. Luggage would be dragged out of the hold and thrown through the security checks where the nosey buggers would search through any case that took their fancy. For all I know, they were trying on women's knickers and stealing cash. The little package I'd intended to bring with me would have passed them by easily enough. No one checks the little shampoo bottles that folks steal from hotel rooms - and I had small collection of those from years ago.

The sub hadn't entered the docks, but tied up alongside and an extendable corridor bridged the gap between the two. It was a non to subtle hint that this was not a city built to accommodate civilian subs. At the end of the umbilical tube I was met by an officer, a lieutenant by the two thick stripes around his sleeves.

"Mr. Hayes." It was a statement and a question so I nodded. "If you'll follow me, sir, we will collect your bag."

If this was the kind of service I could expect now I was being paid by the company, I figured I could get used to it. The lieutenant made a brisk pace through the crowd and it was a challenge to keep up. People seemed to move out of his way and close up on me, though I was barely a step behind. It may have been his uniform, or the fact he was taller and thicker built than me. Then again it might have been the quite obvious presence of the sidearm on his belt. People invite interest, uniforms earn respect, weapons demand fear. He had me beat three to one.

We gathered up my travel bag from the security desk and we hustled onwards, away from the crowds. Down a corridor, making a few turns at junctions, and we were in a different part of the city. The lighting had changed from standard to about one quarter below, a sure sign this was a military base. They seem to have a need for low lighting, either to train their troops' eyes or because they couldn't afford the bills.

At another security check point the lieutenant did all the talking. He handed over his papers and another set which I assumed to be something to do with me. My travel documents hadn't left my pocket. The guard waved us through. The same ritual took place twice more before we joined a wider corridor. The signage suggested we were heading towards the real docks, the ones with the armed subs in it.

Moments later, we came to a halt in front of an impressively large bulkhead door. This wasn't a one person or even two person door. Without much of a squeeze, you'd get the nose of the passenger sub I had come in on through it. This door was guarded by four men, all of them sported a sidearm and a rifle. There were cameras above the door and, judging by the panelling around it, any number of hidden weapons. I smiled as nicely as I could as we approached. The lieutenant showed them the papers again and one of the guards opened the small door within a door that all large bulkheads have. We stepped through and into the docks.

Apart from the domes, and not every city has one, there are precious few large open spaces any more. This dock was one of them. It was enormous and I staggered back a little, feeling a little nauseous. There was space, lots of it. I could see the opposite bulkhead door, but that just meant that it was as large as the one I passed through because it was really just a steel grey smudge in the distance.

Overhead, great tracks carried, suspended beneath them, boxes of equipment back and forth. Long wires lowered the items to the ground where they were needed. The wall to my right was covered in large screens displaying the sub names and departure schedules, ocean currents and temperatures at varying depths, and maps of the surrounding sea floor. In itself it was dizzying, but below these and behind a glass wall hundreds of people bustled around.

To the left was the huge moon-pool. In the beginning, when we had first fled into the oceans, this sort of thing was impossible. The pools were serviced by airlocks and pressure valves ensuring that the water stayed in the pool and didn't flood the city. The big subs would dock outside and the smaller vessels would enter the pools. But, what with necessity being the mother of invention, we had made giant leaps in our control of water and pressure. I didn't have any clue how it all worked, but it did and that's what mattered to me.

In the pools were a selection of subs, from small five or six man patrol ones to the much larger fifty or sixty man ones. The truly great subs, the carriers the military used which would dwarf the one hundred meter or so passenger sub I'd come in on, would tie up outside. There were limits to our technology.

"Mr Hayes," the lieutenant spoke to me for the second time, "may I introduce you to Commander Brannon."

The commander shook my hand then dismissed my guide with a quick salute.

"It is good to meet you," he said to me. "If you would please get on board we can be underway as soon as the final checks are done and your suit is stowed."

"Sorry?"

"We are getting ready to leave, sir." He took my elbow and directed me towards one of the small five man subs. "This the NSU Ashlands, your ride to your destination. We'll be operating a man down as you'll be on board but I am given to understand you are cognisant with these vessels."

I was. I'd been in a few during my military service and had, at one point, be qualified as a crew member, but that was many bottles ago and I wasn't sure my memory would be much use. I settled for a nod and he seemed, if not pleased, then at least a little more at ease.

Walking along the pool deck and sliding down the short ladder into the patrol sub did bring some things back. For instance, how tiny these things were. From the bottom of the ladder it was two steps forward into the cramped command area, one left into the sleeping area and one right to access the engine compartment.

"Mr. Hayes, the documents you need are in the bunks. The trip time is around twenty-two hours. Three men are needed to pilot the sub and we run a split shift with one man rotating out every 4 hours. You are on second shift – you'll be running the Comms panel and safety systems. As we expect to contact no one and have no problems it shouldn't be too hard." He smiled at me and with nothing better to do I smiled back. "Well, I'll see you in four hours."

I took the single step from the base of the ladder into the bunk room and shoved my travel bag beneath the bottom one. The beds were really just shelves covered with a thin blanket. I sat down on the floor, picked up the tablet screen from one of the beds, pressed my thumb to it when directed and started reading about my destination, Calhoun.

There were maps of the sea floor directly surrounding the very small city, more an outpost, and some schematics of the structure itself. It was a simple box with a few bolt-on pieces that weren't labelled with a purpose. There was room, given the military's need to make everyone, apart from officers, uncomfortable for maybe a hundred people.

I could see why they needed a Fish-Suit, especially if the fractures were low down near the sea floor. Though floor would be a little bit of misnomer as it was more a series of jagged peaks into whose narrow valleys the support piles had been driven. The city itself was situated in a much larger valley between two great mountains. If you didn't know the city was there, you'd never find it.

## CHAPTER ELEVEN

The little sub made good time and I did my shift. Really just sitting in the seat and looking at dials and screens which didn't move. I managed to get a little sleep on one of the shelves before having a simple ration breakfast.

"Mr Hayes." The call came from the command cabin and I poked my head out of the bunk area in response. "We are approaching Calhoun."

"Thanks," I said.

"From here on in we are running silent. Can you stow the beds and strap yourself in? The currents can be a little rough." The commander turned back to the front screen and began to flip switches, as did the other crew members. The lighting changed to dull red and the view screen, which had previously shown nothing but the glow of the sub's running lights, and the marine snow that fell through it, went dark.

"I hope you have good maps," I said.

He turned and gave me a big grin before adding, "No talking. Silent running."

There was nothing to see and nothing to do, but enjoy the ride. The bumps, sudden dips and drops were not that enjoyable, though the crew worked hard and well. The silent run in took an hour, give or take a few minutes, and there was a moment of calm as we entered the city's current shadow. The sounds outside the sub changed, from the groan of the ocean to the cleaner sounds of civilisation, as we rose into the small city's moon-pool.

"Mr. Hayes, your suit will be taken out of the hold and put into storage in Calhoun. I've been informed you will be met outside by a member of staff who'll take you to the base commander. We have orders to do a quick turn around."

"Thank you, Commander." I stood, grabbed my bag and

put my foot on the first rung of the ladder then paused. "Will you be picking me up when the job is done?"

"Not for me to decide, sir." The sub commander sketched a quick salute of goodbye and turned back to his crew, issuing orders. At the top of the ladder, the hatch swung open and the face of a young man smiled down at me.

### # # #

"Take a seat." The base commander indicated one of the blue plastic chairs in his office. "The city foreman will be here in a moment and we can begin the briefing."

I took the offered seat and looked around. The walls were painted a dull grey and there was a single desk in the tiny office, behind which the commander sat. The wall had a pin board covered with single sheets full of names and data. There was nothing I could read from where I sat. The commander himself was older than me, his hair was turning grey at the temples and beginning to recede at the front. He had an easy smile and I couldn't find a reason to dislike him straight away. Given time I was sure I'd find one.

"What can you tell me about the base, Commander?" I asked.

He looked at me for a moment then tapped at his computer screen. No city-web or in-eyes here.

"This is a research station, Mr Hayes."

"That sounds exciting. What is it you research?"

"Deep ocean currents and the movement of the plates. We are testing out a new technique for determining the pole shifts using the paleomagnetic properties of the extrusive lava. Not very exciting for a non-scientist." He gave me a smile that said "and that is the official story."

"Problems with pirates?" Any man with a sub capable of carrying a torpedo could call himself a pirate. They were rare in most of NOAH's territory, but in the overlapping zones they were much more common. The tiny corps, or those that struck out on their own, sometimes turned to it as a way of paying the bills. It wouldn't be unheard of for a more organised group to attack a small place like this. And, if this was a Silent City, then it would be unlikely to have an acoustic net set up to detect any incoming threats.

"No more than usual," he said. "We've had reports of some small bands operating in the area but nothing too worrying."

"And that's why the subs come in dark?"

"Dark?" He asked, which told me he wasn't a military man. Curious.

"Dark, as in no lights, no emissions, everything shut down apart from the bare minimum to operate." I watched his eyes as I spoke, was there a flicker in them and if there was, what did it mean? "Small subs use it as a technique to sneak into areas they shouldn't be in or when they wish to remain undetected."

"Really?"

"Yep. You can take that technique and, with some modifications, scale it up to the size of a small city or outpost. No emissions, nothing to give away the fact there is even anything there. They're are called Silent Cities."

"That is interesting, Mr. Hayes. Not sure how it is relevant but interesting. Ah, here is the foreman." He stood from his seat and extended a welcoming hand to the man who entered. I stood and turned as well.

"This him?" the foreman spoke to the commander without meeting my gaze.

"Indeed it is," the commander said and used an open hand to indicate the foreman. "May I present our city foreman, Morris Keller. He will be in charge of the process and oversee it. I believe you have already seen the plans and the nature of the problem we face?"

"On the sub," I said and studied Keller's face trying to see if I knew him from anywhere. My memory came up blank which was a good sign. I stuck out a hand and left it there until the awkwardness of the situation forced him to shake it. "Corin Hayes, pleased to meet you."

There was no recognition in his eyes and I released his

hand. Hopefully, my fame hadn't reached out this far. As I had been unable to travel up until three days ago, I was unsure whether the accident and my part in it was just local knowledge or if it had spread. There would be folks out there who would know my name, but the oceans were big places and there were still lots of people on the planet. Not the nine billion or so that it had once been, too many had died and it would take centuries to recover to that level. If the ocean could support it, that was.

"Yeah." He turned away. "We can get the job done over the next few days. We'll need to check all the supports and then see if this fellow can get close enough. Is there anything on the horizon we should know about, Michael?"

The commander shook his head. "No, nothing. Sooner you can get it done the better, I think."

There was definitely some meaning behind those words, whatever it was eluded me. I did notice the use of first names though. Another hint that the commander was not in the military. I thought back to the docks. Apart from the moon-pool, which was a squeeze for the sub I had arrived in, there were, maybe, only six other subs in their dry docks. They were all small, one or two man. Nothing that looked as though it could put up much of fight. But then, a Silent City relied on not being found, not on the strength of its defence forces.

"Good," the foreman turned back to me. "I'll show you to your bunk. I suggest you get some food and sleep. We'll start early tomorrow with the southern supports and struts."

I nodded to the commander and followed Keller out.

## CHAPTER TWELVE

I woke up with a headache which was really disappointing. I hadn't had a thing to drink the night before. Which might explain it.

My quick tour of the base last night, guided by Keller, had confirmed some of my thoughts. All the sleeping quarters were on the outside of the city and none seemed to have anything but a bed and washbasin in them, certainly mine didn't. They didn't even have windows or small portholes. I put my hand against the outer wall expecting to feel the cold of the ocean leaking through, but there was nothing.

The bottom level was the moon-pool, docks and, above that, a cargo hold. The next level up contained the admin offices, where I had met the commander. The middle level seemed to be labs, but I didn't get much of a look at those. Keller steered me away from the doors so all I could get was a brief glance through a door's vision panel.

The penultimate level, below more crew quarters, was the mess hall and medical bay. Simple ladders and stairs carried you from one level to another. There was no wasting of power that could leak out and advertise their presence; light levels were low, food was a mix of cold and flash-cooked. The cargo and docks would shield the labs and I'd bet the sleeping quarters were lined with insulation.

I threw some water over my face and swirled some more round my mouth a few times before spitting it out. In the mirror, my face looked as though it had returned to normal. It still wouldn't win any awards, but the bruising was mostly gone. I prodded my cheeks and waggled my nose, just to be sure. Not a bad job.

The Fish-Suit skins were a struggle to get into. On top of those, I dragged on yesterday's top and trousers. A simple pair of shoes and a badge declaring my name, and right to be here, completed the outfit.

The mess hall was easy to find, it was on the same level as my quarters. I found a bowl, ladled some of the porridge into it and picked up a glass of water. There was an empty table at the back which I headed for. I didn't make it. Keller stood up from a full table and beckoned me over.

"I'm leaving, but you might as well introduce yourself to the guys." He nodded towards the two men and a woman sat the table. "They'll be out with us today. See you later."

Keller walked off and I sat down. The three stared at me, measuring me.

"So, you're the Fish-Suit guy?" the one to my left said. "I'm Jordon, Rake's the guy with the sea cucumber sleeping on his upper lip, and this is Elena."

I nodded to all three. Jordon was the youngest, barely twenty I guessed. Rake was older, he had some lines around his eyes and that moustache drew your attention away from the lazy eye. Probably why he grew it.

Elena was beautiful. Her dark hair fell long, past her shoulders, and she had gorgeous, bright blue eyes. She was the last to look up from her food and when she did, she smiled. I fell in lust.

"That's me. Name is Corin." I clasped my suddenly shaking hands together and waited for a reaction. As before, I couldn't detect one. "Been here long?"

"Helped build the city, we did," Jordon said. Elena nodded whilst Rake spooned another helping of breakfast into his mouth, leaving enough on his upper lip to feed the creature living there. "Been here since then. Course the ground is always shifting a little due to the ridge, but we factored that in to the plans. We do the maintenance now. Keep it all running."

"So why is it fracturing?" I spooned the porridge into my mouth. It was tasteless. I counted that a blessing.

"No idea. We can't get close enough and the scanners have too short a range. That's why we need you. Can't even get a deep-diving suit close to the area."

Jordon spent the next ten minutes telling me all about how he built the city and nothing about why it was built. It was likely he didn't know. I'd bet that Rake and Elena had a good idea.

"Corin," Elena said as we stepped out of the mess hall. I stopped and turned. The other two kept on walking.

"Yes?"

"Corin Hayes?" It was the tone of her voice which caused my stomach to drop. I took a half-step back, turning side on, and clenched my fists.

"That's me," I said, lowering my chin a little. My ribs still ached a little and I really didn't want to do this.

"I heard about you." She hadn't moved and a quick glance showed that her hands were still in her pockets.

"Really?" My heart was hammering in my ears.

"Yeah." She shook his head a little. "Real sorry about your kid. I got two of my own, though I haven't seen them for a couple of months. Not sure what I'd do if mine died."

"Thanks." I didn't relax. I'd made that mistake before.

"I was on Base 1 when the news broke about the murder. I put a call through to my kids as soon as I could. Just to check. Did they ever catch that twisted son of a bitch?"

"No," I said in a heavy voice, "not yet."

"Ah." She nodded, to herself it seemed. "I shipped out the next day. Anyway, like I said, I'm real sorry."

"Thank you." I let my hands relax, the tension and adrenalin leaving my body. No fight today and I counted that a victory.

"I'll see you out there," Elena said, and walked to the nearby stairs before turning back, glancing over her shoulder. "Maybe we can have some dinner afterwards?"

"I'd like that," I said. Score one for the pity factor. It was about all I had and sometimes it worked.

### # # #

I wouldn't be leaving via the moon-pool. The suit had been

stored in a hastily emptied locker a few steps from one of the airlocks on the same level. It would have been fitted out with all the usual connectors I needed and a store of Oxyquid would have been added.

Back in my room, I emptied my bladder. Needing a piss in a Fish-Suit was never pleasant. I gave my ribs the once over. They would be doing a lot of work today, dragging in and pushing out the Oxyquid. I met my own eyes in the mirror. They weren't rimmed with the red evidence of a night's drinking and I could, for the first time in a long while, look deep into them. There was just the hint of self-respect in them, but I recalled the package that Derva was holding onto for my return and the hint faded away.

I left and headed down the stairs following the signs through bulkhead doors and past the docks. It was a strange thing to walk on floors that did not creak under your weight. Rounding a corner, I stopped dead. Keller standing by an open door, looking into the compartment beyond and next to the door was the airlock. I watched and waited.

The door blocked my view of his actions. I saw him raise an arm and drag something out from the locker. He held it up to his face and rotated the object, examining it. It wasn't hard to recognise, it was one of my suit gloves. I saw him put it back in the locker and step forward into the locker itself, the one containing my Fish-Suit.

My breath stuck in my throat. I could shout out now and challenge him, or wait and see what he did. You didn't touch another man's suit. It just wasn't done. Out in the deep, that suit was the only thing between you and a painful, though quick, death.

Each user was responsible for their own suit. They'd taught us to operate, maintain and fix the things. I could take apart the filter and put it back together before I got anywhere close to putting it on. Knowing how it worked, and that you'd made sure it worked, was part of the process of feeling safer when the Oxyquid was forced up your nostrils and down your throat. When you took that first breath that wasn't a breath of air. When the panic set in you needed to know it was safe, that you'd made it so.

He was in there a while. I didn't like the feeling, so I backed off down the corridor, making as little noise as possible. Ten steps away I took a deep breath and began to sing, quite loudly, a song I'd heard a few times on the clip shows back home. After a two bars, I started walking towards the corner. Within five steps, I heard the locker door shut but didn't stop singing. I rounded the corner and saw Keller stood by the airlock door.

"You're late," he snapped and tapped his watch.

"Sorry," I replied. "Anyway, I'm here now. We all ready to go?"

He stared at me. There was real anger in eyes and I didn't know why. He'd come close to being caught messing around with my Fish-Suit so I expected some anger, as a cover, but this looked genuine. Curious.

"Your suit is in there." He pointed to the locker I'd seen him going through. "You have the code?"

"Yep, got it," I said.

"Good." He stopped and I could see him thinking about his next sentence. "We'll meet on the north side. Don't be late."

"Of course not," I replied.

Keller stood there for a moment, unsure or caught between decisions. A second later, he had made up his mind, nodded to me and left round the same corner I had used.

The four digit code they had given me opened the locker and I dragged the suit out, along the corridor and into the airlock proper. Tapping the control panel, I stopped the outer door from closing. I wasn't in the suit yet and if it closed some idiot might decide to flood it early.

There was just room to lay the suit out on the floor and I began to check it. I worked from the boots up, slowly and methodically looking for tears, holes, scuffs, pinpricks, anything that could threaten the integrity of the suit. There was nothing I could see.

Next the computer and electrics. I put on the gloves and placed the helmet on my head. Flicking my fingers on the touch pads brought up the screen and I set it to run a diagnostic. It came back clean. Everything working as it should.

I checked the activity log and it showed the last time the suit had been used was back at home. It hadn't been booted up since and there was no change in the operating systems or structures.

I took it off again and laid it all out, in place, on the floor, and sat back on my haunches. There was no way to know how long Keller had spent with my suit. He could have come straight from breakfast or got here just before I rounded the corner. Any quick damage would have been visible and he was an experienced operator. He knew that I'd check it thoroughly before leaving the safety of the city.

My clothes, I rolled up and shoved in the locker. In only my skin tight undergarment, I padded into the airlock and began to dress. The same ritual as always, the same order. I wasn't dead yet so I knew they worked. If they didn't I would be dead and at that point I'd have some stiff words to say to my corpse and whoever, or whatever, I met on the other side.

The helmet snapped into place, the system booted up and I connected the tubes. A command issued and I felt the change, the air being forced out, down one tube, and the Oxyquid entering via another, climbing up my legs. On a bright note, I couldn't see any leaks.

"I still hate this bit," I muttered.

## CHAPTER THIRTEEN

"Good day's work," Elena said, over the evening meal.

"I've never seen a Fish-Suit used before," Jordon said, his mouth full of some green leaves. A seaweed salad maybe. Youngsters always seemed to watch their diet more than us older folks. We knew our body would betray us and begin to build fat no matter what we did, so why bother? I kept it down to a minimum, but my metabolism wasn't what it used to be. "What's it like?"

Rake turned his head to Jordon. "Drowning."

"You've used one?" I asked him.

"Yeah, I started the course during my service. I could never get past breathing in the stuff." He shook his head and stabbed his fork into the slab of reformed fish he was eating.

"Takes a bit of getting used to," I said. "It's not for everyone."

"Is it really like drowning?" Jordon asked.

"I suppose it is." Of course it bloody is you little sod, I thought. "Only difference is you know, at least you hope, when you do it the first few times that you are not going to. The Oxyquid will keep you alive."

"What was it like? The first time, for you I mean." Jordon was staring wide-eyed at me.

"Fucking awful," I replied. Rake snorted.

"If it is so bad, why do it?" The boy asked.

"I don't like being beaten by things and once you do it a few times you kinda get used to it. I mean, it's still bloody scary and you still gag and panic, but it's known and controllable." I took a bite of my meal and chewed thoughtfully. Why did I still do it? "And it is still a reasonably rare skill that is in demand. Like today, I can go places your subs can't and work on things that robotic arms just are not capable of doing."

"You didn't do much today," Rake said.

"Nothing wrong with the supports on the north. But then, we knew that. The reports I read on the way in say the problem seemed to be confined to the southern ones. All we did today was confirm those reports," I said without any anger. It was nice to be part of a crew again, even on the outside. I could cope with a bit of bad temper and bluster easily enough.

"So," Elena began, "tomorrow you'll go down and scan the southern struts and we'll all hang in the water column waiting for you again?"

"Don't forget helping me to move from support to support." I gave her a smile and followed it up with a compliment. "Your subs are faster than my suit so the lifts are very welcome. I couldn't get it done without you."

We ate in silence for a moment, chewing the over cooked fish and washing it down with water. This was a dry base, no alcohol anywhere except, maybe, in the medical bay. If things got desperate, I might be tempted by a midnight raid.

"Tell me about Keller," I said. "Has he been here since the start?"

I saw Jordon take a deep breath, ready to launch into a story. Rake shook his head and the air whistled out of the boy's mouth without any accompanying words. I looked between the two of them. Elena just kept her head down and carried on eating.

"What's the story?" I directed the question at Rake.

Rake stared back at me. "No story."

"Tell him," Elena said without looking up.

Jordon took another preparatory breath but Rake cut him off. "Keller wasn't here at the start of the build. He's only been with us a month or two. Hollins was our first foreman. He oversaw much of the build. Team was bigger then, as you'd expect. Anyway, the build went smoothly and most of the others moved on to the next job. We stayed behind, taken on to maintain the base and do... other jobs... they needed doing."

I heard the pause in the middle of that last sentence, but I didn't want to push that just yet. "What happened?"

"About a two months ago there was an incident on the base. The company investigated and though nothing was ever proved a lot of the suspicion fell on Hollins. It got so much that he couldn't take the looks and rumours anymore. He put in for a transfer and it was done in double-quick time. Couple of days after he left we heard there had been accident and his sub had gone down. Everyone was killed."

Elena speared another piece of fish with her fork, but she didn't raise it to her mouth. Jordon sat back in his seat and left his food alone. Rake didn't spare them a glance as he continued.

"A lot of folks thought he got what he deserved, but we don't reckon he did anything at all. Then Keller turned up and took over. The company didn't trust one of us to step up. We think it's because we defended Hollins."

"Life's a bitch sometimes," I said into the silence. "Keller all right then?"

"He hasn't done much to settle in yet. Keeps himself to himself a lot."

"Nothing wrong with that." A small pang of guilt ran through me along with a bigger dose of empathy. Then I remembered the image of Keller fiddling with my suit this morning. "A good boss?"

"He knows his stuff," Rake admitted.

"What had, if you don't mind telling me, Hollins been accused of?" It had to be more than a simple theft or a fight. Construction crews were generally a tough bunch. A little dishonesty, a degree of freedom with other people's money and the odd punch up were expected. They were usually dealt with by the crew themselves, their own little police force.

Rake sat back in his chair and cast looks around the mess hall. All the tables around us were empty. Everyone else, and there were not many in, sat at least three tables away. It was like a buffer zone or maybe, more likely, an exclusion zone.

"Hollins was friendly with one of the science techs. She was a pretty little thing and seemed as taken with him as he was with her." I could have stopped him there. I could guess where this was going. Some men push things too far, too fast and some don't like the word "no". I didn't stop him. "Well, one morning, she turned up for work in a complete state. Black eyes, cut lips and bruises on her arms. She claimed she'd been raped."

"By Hollins?"

"Yeah."

"Did he?"

There was a flash of anger in Rake's eyes and I could sense the other two pull back a little.

"No, he didn't," and the anger drained out of his eyes as quickly as it had risen. "He was besotted with her. He was talking about getting married and having kids. Listen to me, we've been around the block a few times and I am telling you, he wasn't that kind of man."

"You can never tell. It takes all sorts." I raised my hand in an apology as I spoke.

"Yeah, it does. But I'll guarantee he wasn't one of them."

There wasn't anything I could add to that so I sat in silence alongside the rest of them. I wanted to ask them more about Keller. I needed to know why he was fiddling with my suit. Now wasn't the best time. I could tell that from the story and their faces, but I wasn't going to have another chance.

"How conscientious is Keller?" I said. "I mean, does he check everyone's equipment before you go out?"

It was Elena who responded. "He's the foreman. Safety is his look out."

"I saw him, this morning, fiddling with my Fish-Suit," I said. It was as close to an accusation as I was willing to go right now.

"Just checking it, probably," Jordon said. "Make sure it's safe."

Rake shook his head. "You don't touch another man's suit. Just ain't done, Jordon."

I nodded and then turned to the boy. "Your subs are big things. Takes a lot of specialists and mechanics to keep them running. Fixing, checking, fuelling, all that kind of stuff. There are all sorts of computers running checks before you even launch. Fish-Suit isn't that way."

"Why?"

"Being in that suit means you are pretty much on your own. When I was being trained, the first things I had to know how to do was fix it. From the boots to the helmet, there is nothing that, given access to the spare parts, I can't fix. Each suit develops over time to fit the user. Actually, it's probably the other way round. We modify them, bit by bit, to our own specs. There is not a ton of difference, but the way the suit is set up, the UI, the command patterns are as indicative as DNA."

"But you could have someone check it for you. Kind of a double-check," he said.

"I could, but I would then check afterwards. Just to be sure. The training teaches you to rely on yourself. It was important." It was. I can remember it being drummed into me time and time again by the instructors.

I thought he had finished because there was a long pause before he asked the question.

"Why?"

"Why what?"

"Why did you have to rely on yourselves? This morning we ferried you around and if something had gone wrong we would have had you on board or back in the city in a flash." Jordon had an innocent look on his face as he spoke and it took me a moment to realise that he was young enough to have never known about the wars. I was old enough, just. My training had been completed in the waning years of the conflict when there wasn't really much actual fighting. The company politicians were involved by then. Arguing about borders, resources and reparations. However, it was Rake who answered for me.

"Lad, the Fish-Suit was one of the Special Forces during the Corp Wars. They don't give off much electromagnetic radiation and they are quiet to move about in, if the user chooses. They were the sabotage units. Not much use in a fight, but they'd go in and wreck the enemies capability before the battle even started. More civilians died to them than were collateral damage in any battle," he said. "There was a time when they weren't liked by any side."

"Made it hard to get work when I left the service," I agreed with him. "But more and more the Corporations got to see the usefulness of the suits for construction and maintenance of the cities. They are really quite simple devices."

"You think Keller might have done something to your suit?" Jordon asked without guile. The joy of youth.

"I don't think he did anything," I said even though I didn't believe my own words. "I just get worried when folks play with my suit. It breaks the rules and makes me nervous."

"What makes you nervous?" Keller's voice sounded behind me.

## CHAPTER FOURTEEN

The weight of the others' gazes fell on me. It was clear that I was going to get no help from any of them.

"Excuse me?" I said, which bought me a few more seconds of thinking time.

"I asked, what was making you nervous?" Keller said. There was a tone in his voice that hinted he had either heard everything, unlikely as no one else at the table had given a hint that he was there, or he didn't like me. The latter was probably true, but there was an itch, born of long experience, that suggested I had been set up.

"I have to go check my sub for tomorrow." Rake stood up and nodded to everyone, edging out of his seat.

"Me too," Jordon said in a hurry.

I half-turned to get my first look at Keller's face. He raised a hand to stop the two men.

"No need," he said. "It's just me and Hayes tomorrow. All we've been doing is ferrying him about and I can do that easily enough. You three have the day off."

"Thanks, Boss." Jordon said.

"Yeah," Keller said. Rake nodded and left, Jordon followed him, but Elena hadn't moved from her seat. She was staring down at the last of food on her plate. "You all right, Elena?"

"Yes, no problem. Just deciding what to do with my day off," Elena said. I was hoping she was going to stay for the rest of conversation, but after a moment she shook her head, stood up and carried her plate to the counter. With a look over her shoulder, she waved goodnight. Just my luck, another night on my own.

"And now it's just the two of us," I said.

"So it seems. Now, are you going to tell me what's making you nervous?" Keller sat in Rake's abandoned chair directly across from me.

I had to spend all day with this man tomorrow. Through the ear buds I would be able to hear everything he said. Any response I gave would have to be typed or chosen from the UI. The day would go much smoother if we didn't have an argument right now. A subtle lie, a half-truth, an expedient made-up story would be the best thing. I was sure of it.

"Why were you mucking about with my suit this morning?" I heard the words at the same moment Keller did. They weren't the ones I was thinking. It was a toss up to work out who was the most surprised.

"What?" Keller looked shocked, but then I couldn't see my own face at that moment so the coin was still spinning in the air.

"I saw you, this morning. You had the door to the suit locker open and were fucking about with it."

"I didn't do a damn thing," he said.

"It's my suit. You don't touch it. No one does." I could feel the anger churning in my gut.

"Let's be clear here," he said. "I didn't do a thing to your suit. I know how you lot feel about them. I did my time in service too."

"I saw you." It was rising up my throat and I had to swallow it back down. It burned. "I came round the corner and there you were, stepping into the locker."

"Hayes, you are out of line," he said. "I found the door open. I was just putting things back in."

"Bullshit." I stood up, out of the chair and moved around to face him. He stood up too. No one likes being towered over, especially if the one doing the towering is angry and I was. "Keller, I saw everything you did. Don't you get it? I saw you."

"Hayes, get out of my way." He jabbed a finger towards me to punctuate his words.

"Not until you tell me what you did." I knew my voice was getting louder. It's one of those things anger does to you, dulls your hearing and opens your throat. You have to shout just to hear your own words.

"I didn't do a damn thing." His face was red and his eyes were narrowed. "Why the hell would I want to?"

"I don't know. Maybe you hate me."

"Hayes, I don't even know you."

"Maybe you heard about me."

"Now you're just talking shit. Get out of the way or we are going to have a problem."

I didn't realise it until he said it, but I wanted to be threatened. I wanted it to be up front, out in the open. A nice, simple threat. Something I could work with. The suit was fine as far as I could tell, but I didn't like the idea that he had touched it. It was a threat I couldn't quantify, that I couldn't deal with because I couldn't see it, but the spoken word, the promise of "a problem", now that was something I could deal with. It released the anger I had been trying choke down.

A circling right hook, full of justified rage and anger, aimed at his smug, lying jaw. I hadn't planned it. My feet weren't set, my hips weren't twisting into it, my weight wasn't fully behind the blow. I missed.

Keller swayed backwards, just a little, and my fist sailed right past, carrying me with it. I felt his hand push on my right shoulder blade as I spun past. The force of the shove sent me stumbling into the table and chairs.

It was not a graceful descent to the floor. The chairs tangled my legs, the table caught me low in the hips and over I went. I bounced, tumbled, twisted, and ended up half-beneath the table and chairs. My legs were sticking up and I was lying at an angle, face towards the floor. I scrabbled with hands and feet to get myself upright. My ribs hurt.

Realising I was facing the wrong direction, I turned sharply to face Keller. My hands raised and ready to try again. He wasn't there. I ducked and slid to the right expecting to get hit in the back or caught up in a bear-hug. Neither happened.

"As much fun as it is watching you fight shadows, we have a job to do tomorrow. If you have a problem with that, go and see the base commander. Take it up with him. But for the last time, I didn't do anything to your suit. I found the door open and I just put it all back in," he said from the mess hall doorway. "I'll either see you outside at eight am or in the base commander's office later. Your choice."

He left. Just like that. No anger in his voice, but with a choice planted in my mind. A few seconds later two large men, dressed in military fatigues and with weapons drawn, raced into the mess hall.

"What happened?" the one of the right said.

"We had a report of a disturbance," said the other.

"Nothing happened," I replied. The table was out of alignment and the chairs were tipped over on the floor. I saw their gaze take that in. "I tripped."

## CHAPTER FIFTEEN

The outer door opened and I walked out into the deep ocean. I sank straight away. A little thrust from the motors controlled the descent. I kept one hand on the side of the little city as I dropped, just enough to guide my path without using more of the motors.

There were no lights. You wouldn't light up a Silent City for all to see. Light would attract all manner of beasts from the deep as well as the attention of any passing traveller. I brought up the UI and selected the view I needed. A false colour image of the city supports, struts and sea floor flickered into view, superimposed over the dark ocean. The city and seafloor maps had been combined into a three dimensional image that the suit computer could continually update as it monitored my position. It wasn't perfect, but for getting from place to place underneath and around the city it was ideal. Once I got close to the work site I'd switch my lights on.

"ARE YOU READY?" the text flashed up on my screen. A message from Keller in his sub.

"PICK UP. CONFIRM." I chose the response from my menu. He could have spoken his message. Every response I made would have to come from the menu or be laboriously typed. The Oxyquid, which I was forcing in and out of my lungs with my aching ribs, prevented any speaking. You need air to talk. It is true, in the ocean no one can understand your screams.

I guessed he was using the text system to preserve the security of the city. A tight beam laser conveyed the text in a quick burst rather than the longer beam of speech. Across this short distance radio would have worked too, but there would be the inevitable bounce around and leakage. Laser was safer.

I caught the cord and hook as it was played out from Keller's sub and attached it to the eye on the suit front.

"ATTACHED. GO." I sent and within a second felt the tug on the suit. My screen showed that I was rising again and the resistance of the water against my chest and arms confirmed I was moving forward. It wasn't the smooth ride of yesterday. He was probably still pissed with me. As long as we stayed clear of the struts, stanchions and other bits that stuck out here and there, I'd let him work out his anger issues.

"SOUTH SIDE. PREP FOR DROP."

"DROP." I sent back and started to sink again, either the sub was descending or he was playing out more cord. There was enough room for the sub to come down a little way.

"STOP."

I used a little energy from the batteries to spin in place, getting a good look at the small, sharp, valley I was dropping into. A few flicks of my fingers and the view changed, zooming in and out, building up a mental picture as well as the generated one. The image of the valley floor was blurred and imprecise. That was to be expected. They'd dropped the support through it which would have disturbed the floor. At the base of the support, the valley floor, there was just room for both of my feet. The support had started to cut through the valley side higher up.

"RELEASING." I sent, unhooked the cable, and used the motors to control my descent. The valley sides, which I could reach by stretching out my hands, looked rough and jagged. There was a chance that a sharp stone could cut the suit and that was not something to contemplate.

Normally, you'd find the stone quite smooth, evidence of the ocean currents power to erode but not here. The land was too new and still moving. A few hundred years and the little valley I was in now would be another twelve metres west and a little smoother. A thousand years from now and it would have moved sixty metres. Not fast, but sometimes, just occasionally, there were big quakes that shoved the sea floor up and out, further and faster than the reckoned six centimetres a year it was moving now.

I stumbled a little as my feet touched down. The floor was uneven and I had to put out a hand to steady myself. Everything that doesn't belong in the ocean seems to move in slow motion. You had to remember that, even if you moved slowly, you had your whole weight behind it. It paid to be careful.

I flicked the lights on full. White first of all to get an understanding of the location. Then red to avoid attracting too many fish, either curious ones or those that hunted the curious ones. The white light only penetrated about 2 metres, but a slow sweep of the area showed the floor became more uneven further away from the strut. Little and large rocks dotted the valley floor. Some loose and some part of the valley sides itself. The support itself was driven deep through the rock and it was wider than three men stood shoulder to shoulder. I would have to move up and around it to complete the work.

"IN PLACE. BEGINNING NOW." I sent up to Keller.

"ON STATION." Came the reply and I unhooked the tether so I could move freely.

I detached the hand held scanner from my belt and moved up to the strut. Before starting, I made a mark on the strut to indicate where I had begun. The scanner itself was a low power but incredibly accurate multi-spectral device. It measured electrical resistance, magnetic changes, x-rays, anything you could imagine. However, I needed its ultrasound. The emitter, I placed just below my mark and switched it on.

Then I went clockwise around the strut, the scanner in contact with the surface the whole way. The little device sent its readings to my suit and I watched the display carefully. The emitter sent ultrasound pulses through the strut and the scanner detected them. If there were any fractures, the break in the structure would reflect the pulse and that would show up on the scanner. There were defects, just like the other struts. Nothing major right now. In a few years, with a little more movement of the sea floor, they could be significant.

"DROP CAN." I sent and then waited. After a few minutes a large canister came into view, through the red beams, and landed in the valley floor. I scooted over to it and lifted it into my arms. There was some buoyancy to the canister, not enough for it to float, but enough to make it manageable.

Placing it down again at the base of the strut, I took hold of the tube that came out of the top. This was wrapped around the strut, as many times as it would go, and then I entered the command on the canister's keyboard. It flashed up a message confirming it was working and that was it. Under pressure, an incredibly fine liquid was being infused into the strut. Where it met a fracture it would fill in the small gap, making it whole again. There was a lot more to it than that, but I had stopped reading the manual at that point. It worked. That's all I needed to know.

"DONE. PICK UP." The message flashed up to Keller's sub and I used the suit motors to move up the water column and meet the descending cable. Two more supports to go.

## CHAPTER SIXTEEN

We placed another cylinder at the next strut and then I was dropped near the last. Once this had been scanned and a cylinder dropped in, if it was needed, my work was done. The end of my first job on my new contract and, apart from an argument, it hadn't gone too badly. It had been an easy job. Perhaps it had just been a test. I could see why they needed a Fish-Suit. The room at the bottom, near the struts was cramped and getting a sub in close enough would have been impossible. A diver in normal gear would have been crushed by the pressure and there was no robotic arm on the planet that could have wrapped the cord around the bases.

"READY TO DROP." Keller's message appeared in green text across my helmet's head up display.

"DROP," I sent and unhooked the cable. I sank down into another steep valley, the slopes rising either side of me. I turned on the beams and picked out my landing place. The little motors in my pack pushing me a little to the left. A cloud of sediment billowed up around my feet as I touched down. I stood still as it rose around my legs, a mixture of eroded rock, construction dust and dead sea life. It was a bit deeper here than in the previous valley but it provided a level surface to walk on, as long as I was slow and careful. I didn't want to scuff up too much debris. It would settle, but it would reduce visibility.

As before, I made a mark, placed the emitter, unhooked the scanner and set off on a clockwise circumnavigation of the support. The onscreen report showed the same microfractures as all the others had. They had built the city in a hurry and I reckoned the supports hadn't been put in entirely plumb. They were ever so slightly out and that put stress on them all. Combine this with the moving of the earth and fractures should have been easy to predict. On the other side, at least they gave me a job, a chance to earn some money, and to travel again.

There was something different. I was getting a ghost ping from the other side of the support. I'd known it happen before. Usually because of a great big rent in the metal or a manufacturing defect. It was hard to believe that it was the latter considering it would have been tested before it was put in place. Then again, it was unlikely to be the former as this support was taking its share of the city's weight.

"HOLD FOR CAN." I sent upwards to Keller's sub. I'd need to find out what the ghost signals were before he dropped the canister. I might need a lot more than the liquid metal to fix the problem. So I continued on, around the strut, taking the measurements and recording them.

When I found the source of the readings, it wasn't the great big hole I had been expecting. At first glance, in the red glow of my lights, I wasn't sure what it was. I had to edge back a little to get a clear line of sight, not that I could actually see it, to Keller's sub. I sent a short message, I had found something and to standby. I didn't wait for a response.

From the base and running up the strut until it vanished at the limit of the illumination provided by my red lamps was a thick cable. Every thirty centimetres, give or take a few, along the cable was a small box. My hand, even in my gloves, just about covered the rectangular box. I could feel the sharp edges but nothing else. The deep ocean is incredibly cold, somewhere between a bracing thirty two Fahrenheit and positively balmy thirty seven.

I could reach the next box up, but that looked exactly the same. It was a better bet to follow the cable down and that is what I did. At the base of the support the cable disappeared into the accumulated sediment. Before everything had gone wrong, I had been on a few archaeological digs on the sea floor and they all used vacuum hoses. A long tube that sucked up disturbed sediment so that the scientists could see the artifacts they were uncovering. As luck would have it, I had nothing like that with me.

There was a solution, though far from ideal, and I decided to try it. Using both hands, I dug down into the sediment for a few moments until it was hard to see because of the suspended settlement. Then I twisted around, braced myself against the valley sides and ran the motors on my back for a few minutes. They threw water out, as a propulsive force which made my arms ache to hold myself steady, and set up a small current which moved the sediment away. It wasn't ideal and it didn't work perfectly, but it did help.

On the third go, I turned back around to inspect the hole. Through a thin layer of sediment, a set of blinking lights was visible. Once I had brushed the last of the sand off, I could make out a little screen, only a few centimetres across, with a set of icons, one of which was flashing on and off. It looked like a large letter "V" with smaller ones spreading downwards from two sides. I watched it for a few moments and noticed that the flashing was increasing in speed. The cable went straight into the new box so, clearly, it was either the power source or the controller for the other boxes that ran up the support. Curious.

A quick check of the city plans that had been provided did not show up anything. No devices, no repairs and no modifications. It was still unclear, to me at least, the nature of the research taking place in this Silent City, but given its location something geologic was likely. Therefore, these devices were likely related to that and I wasn't sure if I should interfere.

"DEVICE FOUND. CABLE + BOXES. WAITING FOR ADVICE." The message raced up towards Keller's position at the speed of light. Slightly slower than absolute $c$, I did listen a little in science class, but not enough to make a difference. The next thing Keller would do was contact the city and then wait for an answer before telling me what to do. All I had to do was wait.

I waited and had the suit computer run a diagnostic check. Just to make sure everything was fine. You could argue that it was standard procedure. A safety regulation. A result of training. Checking the suit during use was all of those things. But, it was also because I still wasn't sure what Keller had done to it. Being safe was better than being dead. It came back clean. Maybe, he'd been telling the truth and some tech just hadn't closed the door properly. It was, grudgingly, possible.

I waited. The red beams of my lights made the marine snow, that continually fell, turn black. The snow was never particularly pretty. Once you knew what it actually was, any notion of a poetic, pure beauty that snow had held in the old world was truly gone. Oliver Twist was still taught in the NOAH education system. The central tenant being; never ask for more than you have and be grateful for it. Sure, Oliver did all right in the end but look at the hardships, the threats and violence. It was only when a benevolent old man, a sure sub-text revealing that wealth was good and that the corporation would look after you, came on the scene and rescued him that the danger abated.

I waited. It was way past the time needed to check and respond.

"RESPOND," I sent and waited some more. I couldn't talk to the city directly, not from here. My link was to Keller and from him to the city.

I altered the pitch and intensity of the red light. Tried to pierce the darkness and spot the sub. It was pointless, they were not powerful enough.

"RESPOND PLS. INSTRUCT ON ACTION." It wasn't right. By now something should have come back from him. Even an acknowledgment. The battery indicator on the UI showed a good level still. I engaged the motors and began to lift myself out of the valley, up towards Keller's sub. It was possible he had developed a problem.

I was piloting blind. Just guessing he was in the same

place that he had left me and I should, very soon, be coming across the dangling tow cable. Up I went. There was comfort in being under my own control. If Keller was in trouble, he would need me.

The cable wasn't there. I took a chance and widened the laser communication. Instead of the stealthy narrow beam, it was now dispersed. It wouldn't travel as far, but it covered a wider area. If Keller had drifted it should reach him. No response.

Lifting further, I was beginning to get into line of sight of the city's communications. I used the plans and my UI to locate a city receiver and sent a query message. All the operator had to do was measure the angle my laser struck the receiving station and he could locate me, at least enough to return a message. It came through not long after.

"QUERY: KELLER SUB LOC? NO RESPONSE TO MSG," I sent.

"STANDBY."

I hung in the water column and waited some more. A lot of work, civilian and during my time in the military, involved waiting and doing nothing. It spoke to my skill set.

"CONFIRM. NO RESPONSE FROM KELLER SUB. WILL SEND HELP. CAN YOU INVESTIGATE?"

"YES." A man in need, no matter what I may feel about his fiddling around with my suit, trumped everything in the deep ocean. It had to. One day it might be me and I'd be grateful to anyone who came to help.

"STAY IN CONTACT. UPDATE WHEN POSSIBLE. SUBS ON WAY. TEN MINUTES."

Ten minutes was a lifetime and meant they had so few subs that they didn't keep even one on standby. I flicked my fingers in the control gloves and moved power to the engines and lights, switching from red to white. The increased spectrum might pick out more features. I pushed away from the city, seeking Keller's sub.

At first, when it hit me, I didn't realise what it was. The suit was buffeted and a rumbling, grinding moan passed through Oxyquid and into my ears. I sensed it rather than heard it. Then I felt a pulse in ocean. It pushed me from behind, increasing my speed and separation from the city.

The suit thrusters span me around on command so that I could see the city and determine the source. A cloud of sediment was rising up from the depths.

"SUPERSTRUCTURE FAILURE. PREPARE FOR INSTRUCTIONS."

The message flashed up on my screen. It was clear. The strut that I had yet to fix had given way, had failed, and the city was in danger. It shouldn't have failed. Nothing in the scans I had taken suggested imminent failure. Add that information to the pressure wave and you had the cause.

Explosives.

Someone had blown up the strut. The cable, boxes and display, a bomb. Someone had planted it on the strut and blown it up. If I had to guess who, Keller was top of my list.

However, right now, this second, I had another problem. I wasn't too far away from a city that had suffered the explosive destruction of one of its supporting struts. It shouldn't have spelled the end of the city. On the remaining struts, it should be able to survive, but they were out of alignment and already weakened. The city was falling down.

It was falling on me

# PART THREE
# CHAPTER SEVENTEEN

I've never worried that a city would fall on me. It's not an event that I've lain awake worrying about, it's one of those fears you take as read. Sadly, a city was falling on me.

One supporting strut had been blown up, destroyed. An act of terrorism or war if ever there was one. No one blows up their own city. The other struts already weakened by the movement of the ground underneath had not been able to cope with the shift of mass and weight. The city was falling down.

At the bottom of the ocean nothing happens quickly. Again, I had little to compare it with, but the resistance of the water was slowing the process. It was this fact of physics that gave me a chance. I jammed the throttle on my suit motors to full and tried to outpace the city walls as they slumped towards me.

The city displaced water as it fell and that gave me a little boost to my forward speed. Every extra knot would help. Through the Oxyquid, I could hear the little suit motors whining under the stress. There was the terrible queasiness in the pit of my stomach. It wasn't going to be enough.

The display on the inside of my helmet told me the motors were giving it all they'd got and they had no more to give. But they did and I knew that. I suspect my suit knew that too as a warning flared up. Maximum safe levels of power and thrust deployed. It was followed with the warning not to exceed these limits as it may cause the suit to malfunction and put the user's life in jeopardy.

I turned the safeties off and pushed the motors even harder. The whine rose in pitch and my screen flashed up more warning messages and icons than I'd ever seen. There was nothing I could do about them. The one safety feature you couldn't over-ride, was the one that told you all the things you were doing were wrong.

My ribs ached as they pulled in and then pushed out the Oxyquid. I tried to stay calm, but my efforts were largely wasted. Shielded by damaged ribs my heart beat rapidly. Adrenalin surged through my veins and into my brain. I gave myself over to it, every muscle tensed as I pushed the suit motors further - taking power from the Oxyquid pumps and the suit assists. The whine rose to a pitch above human hearing. I could still feel it in my skull. It gave me a headache.

An explosion of bubbles caught up with me, obscuring my vision. They surrounded me, lifted me. I began to tumble, losing my sense of direction. Up was down, east was west, north was up, and down was backwards. I couldn't do a thing to control my path. The suit motors, designed to move water around, became confused by the bubbles of air and gave up. I did all I could and tucked up into a foetal huddle, wrapped my arms around my legs, ducked my head into my knees and hoped.

I was out of the narrow valleys and still in the larger valley which was home to the city. Had been home to the city. This fact was confirmed when I slammed into the rock slope and bounced off. The bubbles and the pressure wave picked me up once more, sweeping me back into the rock again, and again. Even with the padding of the suit, its electronics, its support ribs and motor assists, big purple bruises were sure to be forming. If I survived.

The bubbles and pressure wave had come from the city. Or rather, it had come from the final destruction of the city and the topography of the valley. As the city hit, or even before, its pressure hull would have ruptured. The one thing that kept everyone inside safe from the crushing presence of the deep ocean outside would have split and torn apart. Subs tended to have two hulls, cities had three and some, those whose creators were very fearful of the depths or just sensible, had four.

The Silent City was likely to have only two. It was built in a rush and in secret. It was designed to do a job and do it without drawing attention to itself. Two hulls would be the minimum and quickest to build. One to encase the living area and another to safeguard the first.

As long as the city stayed upright, on its supports, the hulls would hold. But, it hadn't and they hadn't. The first point of rupture would spell doom for everyone on board. Water would rush in through that gap, faster and harder than anything could stop. Anyone caught in that initial flow would be torn to pieces by the pressure. The gap would have widened and the air inside the city would have been compressed as the city filled with water. More ruptures would open as the city continued to fall, twist and contort. Inside the city, the inhabitants would find their eardrums bursting as the pressure intensified. Those furthest from the ruptures would be closing bulkhead doors, trusting that everyone else was too. Survival would be the only instinct. Altruism, the desire to keep the doors open a little longer in case anyone came down the corridor at the last moment, would only kill more. The selfish might survive. The very lucky might survive. But "might" was measured in thousandths of a percentage chance.

And then, with in-rushing water filling the levels, with the pressure outside collapsing the superstructure and with the compressed air inside trying to escape through any gaps or leaks, it would all give way. In the space of a second, the walls would collapse inwards to the centre and the air would rush outwards. The city would be gone and only debris would remain.

The valley would channel that rushing wall of air and water. It would pick up anything in its path and send it careening down the valley like a pool ball. I was the ball and I was hitting every cushion.

I had no control. The wall was coming closer, through the bubbles I could see it. I tried to twist, to hit the wall with my back rather than my helmet. Not a chance.

## CHAPTER EIGHTEEN

"Tyler," I said as I picked up my lunch from the kitchen side, "don't forget to hand in your homework."

"Dad." A word that should be full of love was dragged out into a whine.

"Tell you what I don't want to hear, Tyler? I don't want to hear that you haven't done it again. You get told off, that's your look out," I said. I could see, through the half-open door, Tyler's legs and feet stretched out from the sofa in the main room.

"I didn't have time, Dad."

"You had a week. What more time did you want?"

"I forgot."

"Well, good luck today."

"Dad, can't you help me? It is about the ancient world. You like that stuff."

"I like it because I studied it when I was at school, Tyler. Just like you have to now. So I suggest you turn off the clips and hit the books. You've got time to get some of it done before you leave for school." I headed towards the apartment door.

"Come on, Dad. Please."

"Tyler, I've got to go to work."

"Dad, please."

I paused, my hand on the door handle, ready to turn it. If I was late for work my pay would be docked and the wife would complain. I twisted the handle.

"Dad, please. She'll give me a detention again."

"Taylor, why do you always leave it till the last minute?" The door handle slipped from my grasp. The lunch bag went back on the table and I pushed open the door to the main room. "You can't keep doing this, Tyler. You have to get yourself organised."

### # # #

I woke up. My head hurt. It hurt like hell, way beyond a ten. My thoughts were scattered and forming anything coherent was a struggle. I moved my arm and the pain increased, racing up my arm and smashing into my skull with the sharp point of a six inch nail driven by the full weight of a carpenter's hammer.

My hand couldn't reach my head. There was an obstruction, something preventing me from cradling my skull. I poked at it a few times. There was something familiar, but also a great deal of confusion. Had I slipped on the way into the room? Had the door clattered me around the head or had I smashed into the hard floor of the apartment.

I tried to speak. My tongue felt swollen. It wouldn't obey my commands. In my head I stitched the sentence together, a word at a time. It was short and simple. All I needed to do was say it, shout it, scream it and someone, hopefully Tyler or her mother, perhaps both, would come running.

Nothing. I couldn't speak. My mouth was full of liquid. Blood? I'd have bitten my tongue or cheek when I fell. I spat it out. Least I tried. All I accomplished was to add a pain in my chest to the one in my head.

I couldn't clear the liquid. It wouldn't go. I couldn't spit it out. It was in my throat. In my lungs. Fuck. I was drowning. I was dying. Tyler, help. Nothing. Help me. Drowning. I coughed. I kicked at the floor and tried to drag the obstruction off my face. I pawed at the water surrounding me. Tried to kick for the surface. Tried to swim.

Swim? My head hurt. More than a beating, more than a hangover, but swimming? I wasn't on the floor at home. I hadn't fallen. Tyler was dead, years ago. My wife was gone too.

I stilled my arms and legs, let the current have me for a moment. My brain needed time to think, to remember. The explosion. A city had collapsed on me. All those people would be dead. Why had there been an explosion? Keller. Revenge and hatred forced the pain in my head aside for a moment.

First, the city and the people. I opened my eyes for the first time. The Oxyquid blurred my vision for a moment. I forced my aching ribs to drag in more of the oxygen rich gel and then pushed it back out again. The suit wasn't helping. The pressure ribs, that should expand and press down on my own to assist the muscles, weren't working.

I flicked my fingers in the control glove, the UI flickered on the screen and died. I pushed the controls again and nothing happened. Outside the helmet the ocean was black. I could have closed both eyes and seen more than I could now. The beating pulse of the blood vessels in my eyes would have created fireworks of orange and red blooms. With eyes open, I could see nothing.

By touch, I checked the integrity of the helmet and suit. Considering I had been out of it for an indeterminate length of time, any holes or cracks in the suit would have long ago killed me. It was comforting to go through the rituals. By feel, I knew that I was floating free. Judging by the higher pressure on the front of my suit and only slightly lower on the back I guessed I wasn't moving too fast. I found the switch I wanted at the base of my helmet, at the juncture between it and the pack on my back, pushed it down and held it. This would be a risk. I was kilometres from help, no one around and no way to get anywhere safe, if such a place even existed. I didn't have a lot of choices.

The subtle hum of the Oxyquid filters and motors ceased. A noise I'd long ago grown accustomed to, that had become just background and automatically ignored, stopped. It was unsettling in its absence. The ocean is never truly silent but, at that moment, it was quieter than I ever wished it to be ever again. A quiet that made me doubt my sanity, made my eardrums hurt as they sought a sound, a faint tremor of noise to cup and hold dear.

I was isolated. There was no light to see and nothing to

hear. My brain hurt. Panic set in and adrenalin rushed through my veins. If it wasn't for the faint sense of touch, the feel of my own pulse, my heartbeat in my chest, the friction of the suit upon my skin, I would have lost it there and then.

In the bar I'd been alone but surrounded by others, not truly on my own. The presence of others, even silent and sullen, even without speech or communication, had been a comfort. I didn't realise how much of one it had been until that moment. A drinker who drinks alone is but a moment from death. I felt alone now. There was no world but that of touch. It kept me sane. I needed it to. My brain was starved of input and tendrils of thought waved, lonely, in the silent darkness.

The light came back and I almost cried. It died. And was reborn again. A flicker of an angel's wing. A green light on the helmet screen. Nothing more than single short line blinking in the centre of the screen. It was the world. I watched it. On. Off. On. Off. On. The smile on my face was that of an infant confronted by its reflection for the first time. I wanted to reach out and touch the line. To confirm by touch, the most reliable of my senses and the one in which, at that moment, I placed all my trust, the reality of its existence.

STANDBY...
MEM CHK... COMPLETE
PROC... COMPLETE
STARTUP

Four lines of absolute joy painted in green upon a transparent canvas. The suit came alive as I did. The assisted ribs flexing and taking the pressure off of my abused ones. The sound of the filters kicking in, working up to speed. The beginnings of small currents in the Oxyquid. I calmed my heart and took slow, deep breaths of the liquid.

A few flicks of the control pads and a status check came up on the screen. Both battery and oxygen levels were reasonable. Not great by any description, enough for now and that's all I could worry about. The clock in the lower left, and a quick calculation, told me I had been out of it for about twenty minutes. Nowhere near as long as it had felt, long enough for things to change.

Another flick of the pads and the view on my helmet changed to a map of the local area. It showed the city, still standing, and the valleys surrounding it, the sharp mountains and the fractures that crisscrossed them. My actual position was harder to gauge. Working in a contested zone was never simple. There was no net of sensors, of cables, and signals from which to triangulate your position. Get lost somewhere relatively safe and you'd use the systems the corporation had laid across the sea floor to identify your location. Or, if you wanted to, use your own sonar scans to map the area and compare the topography with the on-board computer. Neither option was open to me, so it was back to basics and guesswork.

The map showed the ocean currents and the instruments on my suit could tell me the speed. A few calculations and some educated stabs in the, literal, dark and I had an idea of where I was. Or, rather, I had an inkling of where the city used to be and that's the course I set.

I had two aims. First, survey the remains of the city in the hopes of finding an intact sub in which to climb. If anything had survived the destruction, it would be the vessels designed to survive the crushing pressure. My second aim, look for survivors.

The first aim had the slim chance of success. The second had none.

I switched on the suit lights and engaged the motors.

## CHAPTER NINETEEN

There was a debris field. Small items had been carried further from the collapse than the large ones. It was always this way, whether the downed vessel was a small two-man or a large passenger sub. Only the size of the debris field changed. The closer you got to the site of the crash, or in this case the collapse, the more debris could be seen.

The first bits I spotted, caught on ridges and spines of valley sides, were clothes and material. I'd probably missed other, smaller scraps, on the way. A red t-shirt here, a pair of trousers there, a uniform jacket further on.

The suit engines pushed me onwards. I kept the white lights on. Giving away the position of the city was no longer an issue and being able to see properly, even in a limited range, was much more important. The falling city might have set off seismic alarms in NOAH or VKING, both of who claimed this part of the sea bed. However, the whole of the Faraday fracture zone was seismically active. The collapse could easily be written up a slight tremor and ignored.

It had made a lot of noise. And noise travelled well through water. Whales could be heard hundreds of miles away. The military, of every Corporation, would have seeded the floor with acoustic sensors. In some areas they formed a net that captured any sound and sent it to bases for analysis. Out here, in a contested zone, there were bound to be a few dotted around.

I'd expect the military on both sides spent a stupid amount of money finding the other side's sensors and destroying them whilst seeding the sea floor with their own. It wouldn't be anything as good as a real acoustic net, but the city's collapse would have been registered somewhere. If it was my side, help might be on the way. If it wasn't, well, then help was still a possibility. Either way, the people of the city deserved some assistance. At the moment I was it.

There was a chance that Rake, Jordon and Elena might have survived. They had subs, they might have been working on them when it started to fall. She would have had... I mean, they would have had time to climb into them. If they'd been close to an airlock then diving into that, locking the doors and pressurising it would have been a possibility. They were constructed as complete, contained units and slotted into the superstructure whole. There was a chance.

I saw the first body. I didn't know who it was. It is hard to identify someone when they lack some of the very things you'd look for. In this case a head. It had been one of the scientists judging by the lab coat that wafted gently in the current. That was just the first of the bodies. On the way in I saw many more.

There were sections of metal sheeting scattered about the valley floor. Cabling, tubes, shattered plastic, wires waving around like tube worms near a vent. In amongst the debris, the people. I could see more white coats and the grey uniforms of the soldiers.

Between a smashed, twisted door and the strangely intact remains of a toilet was a body without a uniform. The back of a shirt was visible and there were only three people in the city who did not wear a uniform, the crew. I dropped towards the body.

The bonus of existing in water is the fact that some objects become a lot easier to lift than they would be in the open air. Add in the extra assist from the suit, not a lot but the Fish-Suit had small motors and an exoskeleton system sewn into the fabric, and many objects became moveable.

With great care, I wrapped my gloved hands around the door frame, avoiding the sharp edges where it had twisted and ripped, and lifted. I was separated from the destruction of the city by thirty, maybe forty, minutes but already the little beasts had moved in. Scavengers pecked and nibbled at the flesh. Others had begun to burrow into the flesh and eat it from the inside out.

They scattered as I moved the door. Some scuttled into a dark crevice beneath another piece of rubble or flung themselves up and into the current, swimming away. The larger creatures, shelled and many legged, had to be picked off the body. Evil looking things that, given the choice, I'd squash out of existence. Though for the one or two that were almost as large as my foot and carried more armour than a combat sub, I would need a very large hammer to accomplish that goal.

I turned the body over, my hands trembling a little. It hadn't been a pleasant way to go. The body was still, apart from the bite marks and burrow holes, intact. The pressure at this depth was the killer. When the city had ruptured, the air inside had compressed incredibly quickly.

In the body, the lungs had been the first to feel the effects. They'd have been crushed in less than a second. The eardrums ruptured. Both would have hurt more than I wanted to imagine. Water would have flooded the mouth. No way to resist. The lungs had filled again, this time with achingly cold sea water. You wouldn't even have the chance to scream or curse your fate. Worse still, your brain would still be operating on the oxygen supply brought to it by your beating heart. Perhaps, if you were lucky, the shock or the collapse of your lungs had stopped your heart. If you weren't that lucky you might live, knowing what was happening for three or more minutes. The look on Jordon's face hinted that he'd died knowing all those things.

I moved on, towards the crumpled city. There were no other lights in the darkness above the site and I scoured the wreckage for an age. There were some places I couldn't get to, but those I could all looked the same. The explosives had done their work. The city was destroyed. No wall was straight, no door was closed, no wiring was attached to anything still working. I found an airlock, it was empty.

The moon-pool was vertical. It was an orifice, an

entrance to the docks and a possibility, however slim, of finding an intact sub. The suit motor guided me in. I had to swim past the remains of two dock workers. They had died with their eyes and mouths open. Faces of panic now frozen in that expression forever.

Any subs I could use would be near the top of the tipped up docks. Their hatches would have been closed and they would have been full of air. They would have survived because they were built to. I held onto the inner rim of the moon-pool and directed my lights downwards. There was a jumble of debris and below that the shape of subs. They'd sunk and I had no way to resurrecting them.

Looking up, I could see absolutely nothing. No large or small subs. No people in emergency suits swimming and surviving. There were, amongst the suspended detritus, the plastic fragments and the sheets of paper slowly drifting apart, small fish that had already moved in to make this place their home. But there were no subs and nothing I could use to survive.

I checked the suit status. Eighteen hours of oxygen left and about sixty percent power. The prospect of floating in the deep ocean for two-thirds of a day, waiting to die did not appeal to me.

Then another light entered the pool. It stabbed in through the ring of the moon-pool and was accompanied by the hum of a large motor. I turned off my own lights and waited.

This could be a friend who'd arrived to help. It might not. Sometimes it pays to wait and be sure before you stick out your arm and wave.

## CHAPTER TWENTY

I watched the new sub nose its way through the circle of the moon-pool's rim. The lights on the front moved left and right, up and down, controlled by the sub pilot. Each light would have a camera attached to it and the view would be projected on screens inside the sub's cabin. They wouldn't see me though. As soon as my lights were off, I had swum over the edge of the vertical moon-pool and clung on there. By moving my head I could see what was happening and duck back out the way if the lights headed in my direction.

The light bounced off the opposite wall and illuminated the newcomer to a degree. Not enough for a stranger to identify the vessel, but for someone else, me for instance, who had been looking for that very sub prior to the destruction of the city it was simple to work out who owned it. Keller.

And that identification rang loud bells in the back of my mind. So loud that they couldn't be ignored and when I started listening I could pick out the tune they were playing. It wasn't a nice one, but it was clear and obvious, and it told me I had been stupid. Keller was new to the city and the crew. The city had only reported problems since he had joined, though some of that could be squarely laid at the feet of the architect, engineers and construction crew for the shoddy build. Once I'd found the boxes, he had disappeared. Then the city blew up and fell down. It wasn't the greatest feat of deduction ever, but it rang true.

Sadly, it also led to the thought that Keller's sub was the only working vessel in the area and, if I didn't want to die out here, it was my ride to somewhere safer. I had to add the 'r' to 'safe' a few moments after I finished the thought. Safety was a relative term.

For the second time that day I took the motors offline.

Keller's sub would be on the lookout for energy readings. It was probably my suit that had brought him here. Even the low level that they put out could be spotted and I wasn't trying to be stealthy. It was either that or he was coming in to gloat over the destruction and death he had caused. A ghoul drawn by death, a vampire by the taste of blood, a shark looking for a meal. Whatever the reason, I couldn't afford to be spotted and I needed a ride. Luck too. Wherever he was bound, it needed to be less than eighteen hours away.

I wormed my way back over the edge of the moon-pool and let myself drop onto the sub. I touched it lightly, using my hands as a guide, and kicked my feet. Keller's sub was one of the typical two-man vessels used in the construction trade. A fat, rounded shape reminiscent of a lozenge or those headache capsules the medics liked to prescribe. There was no bubble of clear material that some subs had to enable their pilots to get a clear view of the surroundings. This one was built to work at depth and in conditions where, nice as the view would be, readouts and view screens were much more useful. It also made them cheaper to mass produce.

At the front of Keller's sub were two mechanical arms that would normally be used to shift pieces of whatever was being built around. They were strong and quite dextrous, as long as the object was in front. They couldn't reach towards the middle or rear of the sub. It was quite possible to use them for other purposes, but they hadn't put those explosives in place. This sub couldn't get close enough and the arms weren't long enough. After all, that's why they had brought me in. A Fish-Suit was the only viable way to get in close and Keller, by his own admission, knew a lot about the suits. Another bell tolled in my head. Maybe he hadn't said how much he actually knew.

Down each side of the sub were the protuberances of sensors, lights and cameras. All of which I had to avoid but were, conversely, fantastic handholds. Also, I had to be careful of the small propellers and motors that gave Keller's sub a great range of precise movement, a necessity for construction. At the rear were the really powerful propellers that pushed the sub through the water. I needed to stay clear of those too.

I found a spot halfway down the sub. A space that was clear enough of cameras and sensors for me to lay the full length of my body against it and still have my feet far enough away from the propellers.

Keller's sub began to back up, out of the destroyed city. In a few seconds he would have passed below me and out into the depths and I would have been captured on any number of cameras that dotted the hull. There was no time to get settled into place with the degree of stealth I would have liked. With no choice, I engaged the magnets in the gloves and slapped them down flat on the sub's hull. A dull clank sounded in my ears. There would have been a similar sound ringing through the hull of the sub. A sound Keller couldn't avoid hearing. Nothing was scarier on a construction site than an unexplained impact on your sub's hull.

Keller's sub came to a halt. It was standard procedure to stop and evaluate any potential problems. I could picture him flicking from camera to camera, screen to screen seeking the reason for the noise. All I could do was hope he put it down to a piece of falling city that had bounced off and sank without being seen. It was a likely scenario. Whilst he carried out his checks, I used the time to get into a better position.

My whole body was now, like my palms, flat against the sub's hull. The only way it would stay there was with the magnets in my gloves, the pressure of the water flowing over the hull and me, and the fact that I had hooked my feet under two of the sensor vanes. I made sure my arms and legs were bent then locked the exoskeleton in place. That would make sure that my arms weren't ripped from their sockets if the water resistance was too great.

From then on I stayed still. It took Keller a few minutes to run his checks before he re-engaged the motors and finished backing out of the city. When he had finally made it out, he executed a simple turn and moved off into the dark. The Silent City, now even quieter, was left behind and with it the first crew I'd felt part of for a long, long time. Left behind too, Elena, only the second woman to show any interest in me for an even longer period of time.

The scavengers would move in and colonise the wreck. In a few years it would be encrusted with molluscs, home to crustaceans and almost unrecognisable. That is the way of the ocean. One disaster is another person's lucky day.

# # #

By the end of three hours my arms were aching. Even with the exoskeleton locked in place, they ached from staying still. Fifteen hours of oxygen left, give or take an hour for exertion and other unforeseen events. I'd be far happier if it gave, rather than took one.

Keller's sub had run dark all the time. No lights and no bursts of speed, just a steady pace. I wouldn't have guessed he pushed it any faster than ten knots, so, at most, we were fifty four kilometres from the city. A more cautious bet would be to place the speed at around eight knots and, therefore, a little over thirty five kilometres.

I was only aware that his destination was in reach when the motors changed pitch. The sub slowed and turned. It held course for a few moments and then the lights snapped on. The illumination was useful as a wall of stone came into view and the sub slowed further to a crawl. Through my helmet, I could see the sub lights play across the surface of cooled lava. Whatever Keller was looking for he found and the sub turned left, parallel to the stone and began to move again.

The lights picked out a cave, or lava tube, ahead and Keller's sub turned into it. The echo of the motors gave the measure of the tube as it widened and narrowed. The light beams showed a relatively smooth surface which hinted that humans had something to do with the construction or, at the very least, widening of the tube.

There were mines on the ridge. NOAH owned a few that I knew about and probably many more that I didn't. The volcanic activity brought up rare minerals from the centre of the earth and encased them in hard basalt. Getting hold of those minerals was a multi-billion credit industry. Corporations guarded their mines jealously. The lack of guards or security systems in this tube meant that this was either an abandoned mine or had been built to stay hidden.

Before long, I could detect another source of light filtering through the water and Keller's sub began to rise. The last thing I needed to be was stuck on when it surfaced. Any guards there would certainly be wondering why there was a man shaped limpet attached to the sub.

Releasing the exoskeleton locks was like learning to walk again. The joy in the freedom of movement in my arms and legs was incredible. Then it was incredibly painful as joints that hadn't moved for hours and muscles which had done little were suddenly asked to perform their tasks. They let me know in no uncertain terms that they were not happy about this. When I shut down the magnets holding me to the sub, it was all I could do to roll off and sink into the dark.

# CHAPTER TWENTY-ONE

The water in the lava tube was clear and the light showed the rippling mirror surface of the water above me. As I fell, I watched Keller's sub rise.

His sub broke the surface and the water foamed. I hit the base of the tube at the same moment and bounced a little. There was no need to engage any motors or attempt to swim. For the moment, I was content to stay at the bottom, hidden from the lights in the shadow of the sub.

The thrumming of his engines changed pitch for the last time and were silent. In their absence, other sounds could be heard. The creak of the sub hull as the lesser pressure let it expand ever so slightly, back into its original shape. The patter of water droplets falling from the side of the sub, reminiscent of the showers in the arboretum, where the last remnants of terrestrial plants were cared for. Beeps and warning noises from the sub as its power unit shut down and the hatch opened. A rhythmic series of metallic clangs from the hull. Then nothing.

I waited in the shadow. One minute. Five. Ten. Fifteen. I had time. The city was destroyed, everyone on it was dead, and the only link to why, and coincidentally my only way back to Base 1 or even my own city, was up in whatever base the sub had brought me to. Somewhere up there was Keller. Once the city's foreman and forever its destroyer. He and I were due a conversation which, I hoped, would be short and mostly communicated through body language. The universal method of conversation, my fists in his face, and he was going to do most of the listening.

After twenty minutes, I rose towards the surface, coming up under Keller's sub, edging around, and peering through the strange refraction of the water's surface. The roof was high, domed and strung with lights. The sub itself was nestled up against the rock and ropes tied it to the dock. I would have to pull myself out of the water to get a good look at the land beyond. Once I did, I was going to be noticed.

No one is graceful, out of the water, in a Fish-Suit and the last thing I needed was for Keller to find me still wearing it. Another disadvantage of being out of the water in a Fish-Suit is the almost total lack of hearing. Sound waves in the sea propagated easily through the Oxyquid and into my ears. Not necessarily understandable or clearly, but I could hear. Out of the water they acted the exact opposite.

No sense putting off the inevitable any longer. Head above water, I pulled myself around the sub to the rock ledge that served as a dock. Through the Oxyquid, another view from a refracting medium, the area looked clear. There was a bulkhead door in the wall, a bank of computers and screens, and a set of gas canisters which were likely there to keep the atmosphere in the base, mine, whatever, breathable. The sub itself had its own supply and carbon dioxide scrubbers. If it lacked oxygen, or nitrogen or any of the other trace gases we needed to survive, the sub could draw it from the sea water itself. There were a few things that subs couldn't produce for themselves, including food, and that's why we had cities and factories.

Most importantly, the dock was clear. No guards and no Keller. The next task was going to be difficult. I had to climb out of the water. You know why a Fish-Suit exits a city through airlocks and not moon-pools? It is easier to step out, into the ocean or use the motors to bring yourself level with a door and step into a city than it is to climb a ladder or, in this case, try to lever yourself out of the water. In the water, the suit, its motors, exoskeleton (such as it was), the user and all the thick Oxyquid that kept you alive, was pretty much the same density as the sea water. It was neutrally buoyant. Out of the water it weighed a lot. Lifting it, and your own weight, out of the water was a young man's game. I wasn't young, but I was bloody determined.

After a few minutes of effort, augmented by the relatively weak exoskeleton, I had managed to get my chest and stomach out of the water. I did not look the picture of grace and beauty, my top half floundered on the rocks and my bottom half dangled over the edge. I stayed like that for a few minutes sucking in the Oxyquid and expelling it with the deepest breaths I could take. Now just to get my hips over the edge.

I heaved myself back up onto tired arms and then wormed, and squirmed, my top half a little further along the dock. My feet scrabbled against the smooth rock, desperate for purchase, something to assist in the process. In the end, I had to go down on one elbow and use the new angle to swing my hips like a pendulum until I managed to get one over the side. From then on it was an easier process, though any crab shedding its shell would look at me and think I had it easy. To be fair, I probably did, but if I caught that crab I'd boil it in water and eat it. Just to teach it to keep its thoughts to itself.

### # # #

The next problem, and choice, was the suit. The readouts showed thirteen hours of oxygen left, which was useful to know, but if I was going to steal Keller's sub then I didn't need it. Actually, I was going to inherit Keller's sub and thinking about it that way made me feel a lot better.

Still, the suit? Back-ups and contingencies. That had been my training and was foremost in my mind. The sub stealing, inheriting, was one plan. The suit was the back-up.

I've no idea who designed the Fish-Suit or who developed it. It never interested me, however, right now, I would sing their praises. If I could sing and if it wouldn't alert whoever was in the base. I giggled at the thought.

I needed to be out of the suit. I haven't giggled in years and out-of-character behaviour, so my training said, was an early sign of oxygen deprivation or shock. Taking a deep breath of the Oxyquid, I held it for a count of five before exhaling. Shock was the more likely of the two. After all, a city had fallen on me.

A Fish-Suit, apart from being quite a simple device, has back-ups and I was intending to use one that I'd never known anyone ever use. On the pack, near the filters, was a compressed watertight bag. My fingers flicked at the control pads in the gloves, searching through the myriad menus, looking for the commands buried deep within. It took three or four goes to find the right subsystem menu and a further minute to read all the instructions on the screen.

Essentially, they told me, all of the Oxyquid would be drained, sucked, from the suit and forced, under pressure, into the watertight bag. A bag that would weigh over 100 Kilograms, my weight and a little bit more. Essentially, it was the normal de-suiting procedure with the added complication of air entering the suit under high pressure. I was encouraged to breathe out as much of the liquid as possible before it began. Survive the process without any breath in my lungs. Easy, if you liked drowning in reverse. Liquid, liquid everywhere and not a drop to breathe.

# CHAPTER TWENTY-TWO

I slicked my hair back. At this point, I usually liked a shower to remove all remnants of the Oxyquid. There wasn't the chance for that luxury. The unwieldy bag of Oxyquid and my Fish-Suit, I stowed onboard Keller's sub. That was going to be my route out of here. I was tempted to take it there and then. However, I had something to do first.

The bulkhead door was closed. After a quick inspection, I twisted the large wheel in the centre and it swung open. As the door moved, I made sure to stay behind it. When there were no shouts of alarm, sirens or running feet, I peeked around the corner. The corridor beyond was long and empty. Strip lighting ran down the centre and doors were recessed into the stone. At the far end, I could see what appeared to be a T-junction, corridors leading off left and right.

I stepped through and closed the bulkhead behind me. Safety first. Anyone coming around the corner would see a man dressed in very little but skin tight underwear and vest. I've never found men in pyjamas particularly scary and I doubt that any guards here would either.

Below my bare feet the smooth rock floor was warm. An unexpected feeling until I recalled that a volcanic ridge was not far away. The first door on my right was unlocked and swung inwards on quiet hinges. It was a bedroom. A very simple metal framed bed with a thin mattress and thinner blanket. There were no pictures on the wall, no washing gear, no clothes on the floor. The impression of it being uninhabited was strong. Apart from the bed, the only other piece of furniture was a chest of drawers. The bottom draw was empty, but I struck lucky in the second. A green jump suit, zipped at the front and free from any markings. I dragged it on over my still damp body. The material clung to the patches of Oxyquid I hadn't managed to clear off.

In the top drawer, when I got to it, was a Bible. It is a strange thing, these different faiths that people put their faith in. Apparently, we were now reliving the flood. Only this time, no single mad man had built a barge to save all the animals whilst letting all those innocent children drown. The book stayed where it was.

The next room was the same, as were the two on the opposite side of the corridor. No personal effects, a single jump suit and a bible. The base had been set up to be a monastery, or a temporary stopover. You arrived, changed, did a little reading, prayed and slept before heading off. Which begged the question, where was the food? The toilets? And the maid who kept all these rooms clean. There wasn't a speck of dust on any surface.

The second question was answered on the next door down. A toilet, which I was happy to use, and a sink where I could wash my hands and drink some water. It was clear and fresh, if a little warm. I took a little time just to run some water through my hair and clear more of the Oxyquid. Watered, washed and dressed, I felt better. Some shoes would be nice, but beggars can't be choosers, just thieves.

At the junction I had two choices. Left or right. There were no handy signs on the wall or the floor. I suspect you either knew your way around or you learned quite quickly. Four beds, two bathrooms, for a total of four to eight staff or Monks, depending on their domestic arrangements, and a maid who might have a room elsewhere. The dock wasn't big enough to have much more than a four-man sub tied up.

I chose left. As before there were doors on either side, but these all had little signs on them to identify their purpose. The first door on the right hand wall had a yellow triangle, outlined in red, with a lightning bolt upon it. The power room. Leaving it alone, I padded onto the next which had a green circular sign with arrows going around the perimeter. In the centre of that sign was the chemical symbol for Carbon Dioxide. The air scrubbers then. Both useful rooms for any city or base to have. The two doors on the opposite side both had signs proclaiming their purpose as store rooms.

The last door, the one set into the rock wall at the far end of the corridor, was the first I had seen with a window in it. Not a large one. It would be a stupid architect who built a large window in a door that might have to resist the pressure of inrushing water. No, this window was small. It was also single glazed, but just that the one pane was the thickness of the door, about fifteen centimetres in all.

There was the ghost of movement over to the left. It was impossible to see clearly through a lump of plastic as thick as that. There were also a million little scratches across it. Quite clearly it had been in place sometime. I ducked below the view port for a moment and thought.

Keller was in the room beyond the door. I hadn't seen anyone else so far so it was likely, unless the other corridor was full of the important rooms, the base was empty apart from him. There were no other subs here, the beds hadn't been slept in and the jumpsuits were ready for people to use, but they hadn't been used. It was an easy conclusion to reach based on the evidence I had. Time, therefore, for Keller and I to have that conversation.

With Elena's face firm in my mind I stood and pushed open the thick door. The room, now exposed to clear view, was a mess hall. Two rows of tables, regularly spaced, and a kitchen area opposite the door I'd entered through. The walls were bare but there was a cupboard full of cutlery, plates and cups at the far end of the room.

"Keller," I said as calmly as I could, "you and I need to have a talk."

The door closed behind me as Keller, who had been sat at one of tables, his back to the door, slid the chair back and rose to his feet. He was taller than I remembered and wider. I also noted that he seemed to be wearing a base standard jump suit.

"I'm not Keller," the man said and turned to face me. He was right, he wasn't Keller.

"Sorry, wrong room." I reached for the door. He headed towards the kitchen and what looked like a fire alarm button. "Shit."

He was a big man and moved with the slow confidence of big men. It was an arrogant walk. It was telling me there was nothing I could do to hurt him. He didn't even look at me. That made it easier. I ran across the room and leapt up onto his back.

Nothing would have pleased me more than to have knocked him down and finished him off with a swift kick to the head. To my painful regret, that didn't happen. The big man staggered when I landed on him and I wrapped my arms around his neck, squeezing as hard as I could. He took two more halting steps, regaining his balance before standing up straight and grabbing my arms.

He pulled and I resisted. The sad fact was, he was stronger than me and, centimetre by centimetre, he dragged my arms from his neck. With a final shrug of his shoulders, he deposited me on the floor. I scrambled backwards and up onto my feet as he turned around.

"You shouldn't have done that," he said.

"We all make mistakes," I said, wincing at the renewed pain in my ribs.

He rolled his shoulders and closed his hands into great fists, raising them in front of his face. "You certainly have."

A big man will generally beat a small one and, in my experience, then continue to beat them until the smaller man is black, blue and unconscious. He stomped towards me. I backed up, pulling one of the tables in the way. It proved a minor inconvenience as he lifted it with one hand and sent it skidding across the floor.

He lunged, both meaty arms outstretched and I had nowhere to go. I tried to kick him in the fork of his legs. Already falling backwards, all I managed was to graze his thigh. His arms clamped around me and he lifted me off the floor in a bear hug. My ribs screamed in agony. I had one arm free, the other caught by my side.

The big man began to squeeze and for the only time during our acquaintance I was glad he was so muscled. All of those bulging muscles in shoulders, biceps and chest actually prevented his arms from contracting all the way. It was still bloody painful, but I could, at least, gasp in short breaths.

I stuck my free palm below his chin and pushed backwards. My arm against his neck and I was winning, just. His head tilted back and visible now was the grimace of effort on his face. My panting breaths were not providing enough oxygen to keep this up for long and it wasn't doing anything about his arms. I extended my arm as far as possible, arching my back against his arms. When my arm was at full extension, I held it there for a second, then let go.

His head shot forward now the resistance was gone. At the same moment I snapped my head down, leading with my forehead. I hit him where I'd hoped, right on his nose. The cartilage and flesh collapsed, warm blood, his blood, splattered over my cheeks. I hit him twice more, this time with the elbow of my free arm.

The big man's head bounced off a table as he fell. It was only when he hit the ground that his arms relaxed their hold enough for me to struggle upright and stagger to the wall. He looked unconscious or dead. Either one worked for me. Blood still poured from his nose, but his arms didn't rise to hold his face.

When I had my breath back, I bent down to check his pulse. It was there, but by the time he woke there was every chance he'd wish he had died. The broken nose would be painful and so would the lump on the back of his head from the table. I watched him for a moment, considering. If I'd been wearing shoes there would be a strong temptation to boot him in the head a few times just for the purpose of security.

"Bugger." For a big man he had tiny feet. His boots clattered into the bin. I took hold of his shoulders and dragged him into the kitchen area, out of sight. In the cupboards behind the counter was a selection of food and it was lunchtime.

## CHAPTER TWENTY-THREE

I left the wrappers and cutlery on the table then went back to check on the big guy. He was lying on the kitchen floor and still out cold. My ribs hurt. But, all things considered, I felt that I'd come off the better. The possibility that Keller was not alone on the base was higher than I had given credence. There could be a few more here, or it could have just been the big man and Keller. The sub in the docks was a two man and that made sense. However, a false assumption had led me into trouble once and, from now on, it would pay to be careful.

The view through the scratched window in the main door showed the corridor was empty, so I crept out. Fed, but aching and without shoes. Bypassing the first four doors, I stopped at the intersection and peered around the corner. Empty. So I continued straight on down the right hand corridor.

Here the doors were offset from each other, completely at odds with the other corridors. On the right, as I walked, the first door had a window through which the room appeared to be used for meetings or conferences. A large round table surrounded by eight chairs and a large screen at the far end. Other than that it was empty. I moved on.

The second door, on the left wall, was thicker than the others. A proper bulkhead door. All thick metal and no viewport. I put my hand against the locking wheel and gave a gentle push. It was locked and, for the moment, I was content to leave it that way. There were three other doors ahead, none of them bulkheads and more likely to have rooms beyond.

The next door, on the right, was unlocked and I went in. As everywhere, the lights were already on and that made my rooting around easier. It was set up as a science lab. Large metal tables down the centre covered in microscopes, glass vials, grey trays full of bits of rock and other specimens. The right hand wall was all filing cabinets and clear, locked, cupboards full of chemicals. The back wall was covered in view screens and precisely none were switched on. Evidence of a deserted base perhaps?

The left side was lined with desks. All had notepads and computers with small screens upon them, and all were neat and tidy. Not in use. I picked at a few keys to see if the computers had been left on. They hadn't. A quick inspection of the filing cabinets only told me what I already knew. It was science lab and looking at rocks. Beyond that all the arcane language used might as well have been magical spells for all the sense I could make of them.

Opposite the lab, the next door was a storeroom for more science equipment. I didn't bother going in. The room, through the window, looked a mess. Next to the storage room was a door labelled 'Server' through which a quick peek revealed the computer servers for the base.

The last door on this corridor was at the far end and again it looked empty. It was clearly the command post for the little base, being relatively large, and around the walls were six desks and a large bank of screens with readouts above them. These were on and working. The centre bank of screens seemed to show an ever updating graph of temperature variations and readouts concerning mass, density and oxygen concentrations of a location called Deep One. The screens to the right showed similar readouts for a place called Deep Two.

My first thoughts were that the data related to two bases, Deep One was this one and Deep Two was somewhere else close by. The left hand screens didn't solidify that guess in anyway. However, they did answer a few questions I'd developed since I'd entered the base on the back of Keller's sub.

Four beds, eight chairs in the meeting room, three desks in the lab, six in the command centre and a mess hall that could cater for twelve easily. Everything had been built out of proportion to the number of beds.

The screens to the left were live feeds from cameras. I couldn't see anyone moving around in them, but they did show another dock. A much larger tunnel and dock area that could easily accommodate a ten, or even a fifteen, man sub though, more likely, a small cargo sub. Next to the docks, a large tunnel and I could just make out the large bulkhead doors about five metres into it. The other screen showed another mess hall and kitchen area.

Perhaps, Deep One was joined to Deep Two. It seemed a logical conclusion and answer to my questions. Deep Two was a mine and Deep One, if I was correct, a lab to check rocks for something or other. My knowledge of geology was fuzzy at best. Not a major mining operation, but small scale could often float beneath the notice of the big corporations.

It still didn't tell me why Keller had infiltrated a Silent City, with all its paranoid security checks, and destroyed it. On second thought, those security checks seemed a lot less paranoid now. Someone was going to lose their job over this when the news got out. When I got out and told someone.

I checked the corridor, paranoia creeping into my behaviour, making sure it was empty, before I sat down at one of the desks and flicked the computer screen on. It asked for a password which I couldn't give, so I settled for rifling through the drawers, one on either side of the desk. I found a few pencils, all worn down and in need of sharpening, and some paperclips. Many of the clips were bent out of shape, some straightened, some curled and turned into knots. The sign of a worker with time on their hands and a boring job. Or maybe one who didn't take their job too seriously, because in the other drawer, underneath the pencils and other stationery supplies was, taped to the bottom, a list of random letters and symbols. All those at the top of the list had been crossed out leaving the one at the bottom unmarked and easy to read.

The computer accepted the password without complaint

and I was in. The first few minutes were spent going through the worker's personal documents. There were some pictures of family. A man, woman and small red-headed child. It wasn't clear which one of them worked at this desk, though the child did have the spark of intelligence in her eyes. There were a few personal messages too, nothing racy or even interesting. I skipped past them and started to look through the files for information about the base.

The first few files I pulled up were long lists of replacement parts for mining equipment, for computer spares and office supplies. The paperclip budget wasn't as high as I'd suspected. I moved on. A few spreadsheets of mining yields were next. The quantities were small, confirming my belief in that regard, and, judging by the dates, it was an intermittent operation. They'd mine for a week or two and then nothing for a month. Round and round it went in the same pattern. The furthest the dates went back was four years. They'd been here before the city and defended their claim it seems. To what, I hadn't yet discovered. I sat back in the chair and pondered the screen.

Sadly, I didn't hear the door open and close. I did hear the soft tread of feet as they came up behind me. Rising from the chair, I twisted to face whoever it was.

All I saw was a heavy wrench swinging at my head and all I knew was I couldn't dodge it. My last thought, before it all went dark, was about Keller's hair colour. It had changed. Then the wrench hit my head and my head, along with the rest of me I suppose, hit the floor.

# PART FOUR
# CHAPTER TWENTY-FOUR

I woke up. My head screamed. It shouted in my ears, dug fiery fingernails into my skull and ripped chunks of flesh and bone away before piercing the grey matter below with a million ice cold daggers. I passed out again.

### # # #

I woke up. My head felt as though a dozen whales had fallen on it and were, even now, slapping me with their massive flukes, making it clear how much they viewed the whole thing as my fault. The room started to darken again. I fixed my, admittedly blurred, gaze on a grey object in the distance and took a long, very careful, deep breath. The dark lightened so I took another and then another.

Each heartbeat pushed a torrent of blood up through my neck and the pressure threatened to blow my brains right through the top of my skull. The floor was comfortable so I stayed there.

### # # #

For the third time in... actually, I have no idea how long, I woke up to a headache. My vision was clearer and I could feel the pain in other parts of my body. Surely that was a good sign. It meant that, although my head hurt it had now given up its top spot and let other bits take the lead.

I lifted a hand to my head and almost passed out again. Red and orange spots exploded behind my closed eyelids. I had to take a few deep breaths, letting the blood return to the parts of my body it was supposed to be in. It took a few more breaths before I felt able to move again.

With a careful fingertip, I probed at the large lump on the side of my head. There was a crust of blood and my hair was matted together in great clumps. The lump itself felt enormous, like someone had stuck an anvil on the side of my head and were repeatedly bashing it with a heavy hammer.

The blurred room struggled into focus and that didn't help matters. It was a box, twice as long as I am tall and a little wider. In the far corner, a low chest of drawers, metal ones, of the type mechanics use to keep their tools in and organised. That could be handy. The door I noticed, with no surprise whatsoever, was closed. On a bright note, there was a handle on my side of the door, but depressingly, below that a lock.

The rest of the room was bare, empty. No help. Flat grey walls merged into the sprayed cement floor and ceiling. No joins, no weak points. A few pipes, painted grey, came into the room, passed over the door and out through the opposite wall. Whoever did the interior decor was clearly paid too much.

Nothing to see, so I listened. The thrum of power generators vibrated through the floor, I could feel and hear them. Nothing else, and no chance of learning anything new from the floor. I'd have to move and wasn't looking forward to it.

I took a deep breath, my ribs hurt. Rolling over, onto my side, I pushed myself up onto my knees. My head felt heavy. It wanted to fall off my shoulders and roll across the floor. I stayed on my knees until the room came back into focus and my stomach stopped threatening to throw up the food I'd eaten. When was the last time I had eaten? Crap, now I felt ill and hungry.

My balance was not the best, but I managed to stagger over to the door and try the handle. Locked. There were two likely outcomes. First, Keller had decided that I wasn't going anywhere and had locked me in this room until I died of starvation, asphyxia or boredom. Or, the second option, and my preferred one given the circumstances, Keller had dumped me in here as a holding cell and would be returning at some point to... well, now, here was the issue. What would he be returning here to do? Kill me or set me free? Sadly, it was more likely to be the former.

I needed to get out and had nothing on me to help. That meant whatever was in those mechanic's drawers, by the far wall, were it. A laser cutter, a chainsaw, even a great big hammer would be something. With hope in my heart and holding my head with one hand, to make sure it didn't fall off, I staggered over to it.

I checked the drawers, one at a time and then spread out all the finds on the floor to consider my options. There were not many. Certainly no cutting tools, not even a pair of scissors, and no hammer. In fact, the only things I found were a monkey wrench, no blood on this one, and a strap, one those things people used to tie objects down with. On one end of the strap was a metal ring.

What was I supposed to do with these? Make a primitive weapon by attaching the strap to the wrench and swinging it about? Wrap the strap around my head, to keep the hair out of my eyes, and use the wrench as a club? I knew that worked. I had the lump and the headache to prove it. Both pointless ideas.

Another check of the drawers just proved that I had done a thorough search the first time. I ran my hands around the walls and door, just to see if I had missed a weak spot or, and I knew it was desperation thinking, a secret door. There wasn't one.

Me, a strap and a wrench. A mostly empty room and a door locked from the outside. I was trapped. No two ways about it, the only way that door was being opened was by someone on the outside. I had to hope that someone did, and I had to be ready to do something when they did.

I sat back against the wall, opposite the door, and pondered. A little time later, I had an idea. Not necessarily a good one, but it was the best I had.

My head hurt, it throbbed, ached and sent the occasional wave of pain through my skull. None of it mattered. The pain meant I was, for the moment, alive and it was better to suffer than to be dead.

The metal drawer unit was heavy. Even empty, it was hard to move. I scraped it across the floor, wincing at the noise it made, certain it would draw Keller back to the room. However, I did not have a choice. Staying in here to die was not how I wanted to go.

Once it was in position, I clambered on top and stood up. My legs hurt, everything hurt, and the increased altitude made my head dizzy. I placed my hands on the wall and waited for the moment to pass.

The strap, about two centimetres wide and made of tough plastic strands woven together, I wrapped around the lowest pipe, just next to the hexagonal nut. The pipe was hot and I had to wait to see if the it would melt the plastic. It didn't, which I suppose made a lot of sense. Who makes straps that melt when they get a little hot? No one, that's who. The end of the strap passed through the ring and I pulled it tight.

The next task was to undo the nut with the monkey wrench. It resisted at first, and it took all the strength I had left in my arms to get it moving. It squealed and complained when it finally gave way. When a whistle of steam started coming from the loosened nut, I stopped and reversed the rotation a little. The whistle died away.

After climbing back down and resting for a few minutes, I dragged the drawers back into the corner where they had come from.

All I could do now was wait. Well, that and hope.

# CHAPTER TWENTY-FIVE

The scratching of the key in the lock snapped me out of the daydream. A shame really, Elena was just about to take her top off.

I rolled and scrambled to my feet, took quick steps over to the door and grabbed the dangling strap. There were a few clunks from the lock as the tumblers moved and the block slid back. The door opened inwards, shielding me from sight, and I held my breath.

At the sound of the first footstep into the room, I took a strong hold on the strap, wrapping it around my fist. On the second click of a heel on the concrete floor, I pulled hard. All my weight dragging the strap towards the floor. The edge cut into my palm, but I couldn't stop. It had to be done now and as quick as possible. I could hear the scrape of a shoe as Keller turned and an indrawn breath as he prepared to speak.

The pipe and nut gave way with a metallic snap that echoed in the small room. It was followed by a serpentine hiss and a scream as the superheated steam sprayed down on to Keller. The door kept me safe from the initial scalding and as the steam billowed around the door it had already cooled enough to be painful but not dangerous.

Keller, by the screams and thumps, was in great deal of pain, something that I felt no sympathy for. The urge to race round the door and put a few well-placed boots into any soft parts of his body I could find was great, but I had to wait.

The steam was still screeching out of the pipe. There had to be an automatic cut off somewhere in the system. A sensor that said, "hey, the pressure in that pipe has dropped all of sudden. There must be a problem. Best shut it off and send a workman to fix it." Something like that.

A minute later the steam stopped. By then, I was soaking wet and, no doubt, my pores were open. Some people pay a fortune for this kind of beauty treatment. I got mine for free, if you disregarded the bruises, headache and all those dead people.

I gave up trying to dry my hands on my sodden jumpsuit and settled for a firm grip on the monkey wrench. Keller had stopped screaming a few seconds ago and I could hear him moaning in agony. The steam misted the doorway and it was a careful few steps through it until Keller's boots came into view.

His legs were jerking and kicking at the floor. The mist cleared further and more of Keller came into view. He was face down on the floor, hands clasped to his head, chest heaving, and little childlike whimpers escaped between his fingers.

At that moment, in that second, I wanted to say something about all the deaths he had caused. All the suffering the people in the Silent City had gone through. How this was his just desert, his justice, the punishment for his crimes. I wanted to shout at him. Scream at him. I couldn't. So, I hit him with the wrench. Just below his ear, not hard enough to kill, I hoped, but enough to knock him out. It was almost a mercy.

The mewling stopped and much of the twitching agony left his body. Not all, even unconscious, his body still felt the burns and scalds. I knelt down and turned Keller over.

The man's hands were blistered. Some had already burst and a clear liquid, the serum, wept from those wounds. With care, I pulled his hands away from his face. Even knocked out, he offered instinctive resistance.

Vomit raced up my throat and splattered onto the floor. Keller's eyes were gone. I mean they were there, but boiled, exploded, destroyed. A runny, gooey, mess. The exposed skin had split, but blood had not run. Instead, the very edges of each split had been broiled and sealed in great lumpy, splotched lines and curls. The tip of his nose had dissolved and below it, his lips had peeled back to reveal shockingly white teeth. No one would recognise him.

The decent thing, the human thing, the ethical and moral thing to do, would be to put him out of his misery.

I left him.

### # # #

The corridor was empty when I stepped out. To my left, the control room where I had been hit and to the right was the route to Keller's sub. And I would need that sub if I was to going to get back home. The suit would never get me that far.

Still shoeless, I crept down the corridor past the lab and meeting room to the left hand turn that led to the docks. A quick glance round the corner showed it to be likewise empty and the docking bay door was closed, just as I had left it.

As far as I could figure, the base should be deserted. The cameras had shown nothing, only Keller and that large fellow, who was hopefully still unconscious, had been in the base. I should consider myself lucky, I suppose.

Slipping round the corner and keeping my back against one wall, I started down the corridor towards freedom. Despite my assumptions, there remained the need to be cautious. Check, double-check and when you're really sure, check again. That's what I was taught when I learned to use the suit and right about now it seemed a safe way to operate.

I checked the first door. It was quiet and when I peeked into the room it was the same undisturbed bed and chest of drawers I had seen on the way in. Two quick steps across the corridor and I ran the same check on the door opposite, to the same result. Two more to go, and I moved forward.

The door ahead, on my right, opened and green jump-suited figure stepped out. Her hair was mussed from sleep and her reactions were slow. It was the perfect opportunity to take her out. A simple couple of steps, push her into the room, hold her down and tie her up with the bed sheet. From there, just move on to the moon-pool, steal the sub and head out. Easy.

The thing is, I didn't move. I just stood there. In shock. How in the hell was she here? She was dead. I know she was.

"What are you..." her voice petered out.

"I was about to ask you the same thing. You're dead," I said.

She looked around, back into the room she had come through, behind her to the closed doors, both large and small, to the moon-pool and then her gaze returned to me. I couldn't read the look in her eyes with any precision. Confusion was my best guess.

"I'm not dead," she said.

"We have to get out of here." I regained power over my legs and moved forwards. "Keller's dead. I killed him. Just now. We have to go. There could be more of them. Why did he bring you?"

"Keller?" her voice trembled.

"Dead. After he destroyed the city, I searched the ruins then hooked on to his sub. It dragged me here. We have to go. I don't know if there are any more of them around." I started to drag her down the corridor, but a thought occurred to me. "Elena, why are you here? What happened?"

"Happened?"

"How did you get here? Why did Keller bring you?"

"Corin," she cast a worried glance over her shoulder, "let's get out of here. It was horrible. I'll tell you when we are far away from here."

The small door within the large dock door opened on its silent hinges. I motioned Elena to wait, hefted the wrench and ducked through. It was empty apart from the sub and, after closing the door behind Elena, I told her to get in whilst I retrieved my suit.

In hindsight, I should have asked her to help me move it. That thing was bloody heavy.

# CHAPTER TWENTY-SIX

Once the little two man sub had cleared the tunnel, I killed the lights. The world went dark and my eyes had to adjust to the dim light from the subs control panel. A few flicks of my fingers and the course was set, back to Base 1 and home. With a girl in tow. How was I going to explain that to Derva? Why did I think she would care?

"91 hours," I said.

"Till what?" Elena answered.

"Until we are back in a NOAH city and safe." I slid the pilot's seat back a little further, getting comfortable and settling in. Keller must have had short legs. "Why did he bring you?"

"Keller?" she said.

The subs green lighting changed the tone of her skin and hair. It did not steal her beauty. I could see her, in profile, focusing upon the navigation screen in the middle of the console.

"Yes."

"He told me he needed some help on the sub. When the city started to collapse, he turned the sub around and ran for it. I'm not sure what else he could have done. We did go back and search for survivors." She met my eyes at that point. "They are all dead aren't they?"

I nodded. "And then?"

"He said he knew of a private company base not too far away. It had been set up a few years ago and wasn't used much. The city kept a watch on it, he said, but they hadn't shown any knowledge of us."

"You know he destroyed the city? There were explosives on the supports. I tried to contact him, but he didn't respond. The city tried too. Nothing."

"How do you know he set off the explosives?" she

asked.

"Who else? He didn't like it when I turned up. We had a fight the first night, in the canteen. And I caught him fiddling with my suit. No one touches another's Fish-Suit. I think he knew that I would find them and had to move his plans forward," I explained.

"But he took us back in to find survivors," she said.

"No. He took you back in to make sure that everyone was dead." I shook my head. "I think he expected me to have been killed in the explosion or the collapse. Even if I hadn't, the Fish-Suit is not enough to survive out in the open ocean for long. It hasn't got the reserves or the range."

"Keller was trying to kill everyone?"

"It seems so. Which leads us back to the reason he brought you along. Why?"

"To help him on the job. That's what he told me," she replied.

"No, that doesn't make sense." I tapped at the console, achieving nothing but giving my brain time to work. "How was Keller before I turned up?"

"He wasn't there long. After our old foreman left, you know that story?" I nodded in response. "Of course you do, sorry, not thinking straight."

"What was he like?"

"He was all right, a bit creepy sometimes, but you know how the gangs are. It takes a while to settle into a new one," she said.

"Creepy. How?"

"He kept talking to the others and not me. But I would catch him looking at me sometimes. I thought he was just shy or something. Men can be like that, you know. Some are all confident and talkative, others are just quiet and shy. You see everything, right up front, which is fine because you know what you're getting, with the first lot, but you have to dig for the gold with the second. Gold you've found yourself is worth a lot more than the stuff that is thrown at you."

I let her talk for a while, though I wasn't entirely sure who she was talking too, me or herself. When she paused, I prompted her with Keller's name.

"He came to me in the morning. Before you'd left and said he'd like me on the sub to help him move you around. You know, one to drive and one to operate the winches and cables. That's it."

"He didn't say or do anything else?" I asked.

"No."

"What about when you got to that base? Anything seem strange then?"

"Not a lot. It was just a small operation. I didn't see many people. Just Keller and one other man, I never got his name, and a few of the miners from the lower levels. I still can't believe Keller did that." She shook her head, dark hair swirling about her face for a moment.

"Anything else? Did he make a pass?"

"He was a little awkward when he showed me the room, the one you found me coming out of, but I thought that was just delayed shock." Her hand reached out and took mine, softly enfolding it. "Do you think he was going to hurt me?"

"I don't know," I said and squeezed her hand in reassurance. "Any man that can destroy a whole city could probably do anything."

I checked the readout again. The sub was on autopilot, following a route back to Base 1. The seascape around here wasn't documented well enough to stick to the canyons and avoid the ridges, the way I would have preferred. Instead, I'd had to rise up the water column to be clear of the peaks and set a straight course. Once we got away from the volcanic area, the maps would be more reliable and I could lower us again.

"This is not going to be comfortable," she said.

"Does the sub have a bunk or a head?" I asked.

"It has a single hammock that Keller said could be strung up and the head, well, its got a receptacle one just behind the bulkhead. Not pretty or private," she said.

"Great." She was right, this was not going to be a comfortable trip. 91 hours in a tiny tin cigar. One bed, hammocks always give me back ache, and a toilet which was not really designed to be used. I checked the air scrubbers, just to make sure they were working. Rogue smells in the cabin had nowhere to go if the scrubbers didn't work. Chalk up one piece of luck on my personal scoreboard, they were, according to the computer, in perfect order. "I'll string up the hammock. Do you think you can search for any food and water? I reckon he must have brought some. Just in case it didn't all go quite to plan."

I watched her shuffle out of the chair and start to search. The green jumpsuit pulled tight in all the right places, shame about the colour. I had to take a deep breath and remind myself that this wasn't the time.

The hammock was packaged in a tiny little nylon bag and next to that a first aid kit. I opened the kit, dug through it to find the painkillers and popped two, dry swallowing them. The nylon bag, I unzipped and pulled the hammock out.

A lattice work of plastic coated cord that would cut into your back as you tried to sleep. I'd slept in a few like it during my short military career, usually on subs a bit bigger than this one. Having said that, I was normally surrounded by a bunch of other men and women trying to get some sleep, belching, scratching and farting the whole night through. Not my happiest memories.

The first string I wrapped just above a nut on the one of the pipes running floor to ceiling and the second I tied around a pipe opposite. The sub was not as wide as I was tall, comfort was not going to be forthcoming.

On a bright note, Elena had found some food and water. Not a lot, but it was better than nothing. We sat in the seats and chewed at some of the pickled seaweed and lab grown beef jerky, sipping a little of the water to wash it down. Keller had had strange tastes.

Between the groaning sounds of the hull and the soft whir of the motors, the ping from the comms panel was shockingly loud.

## CHAPTER TWENTY-SEVEN

I scrabbled back into my seat. The message light was blinking. This was not good news. No one knew where we were. This had been the only sub in the base, the city was destroyed, and Keller was dead. The big guy I'd knocked out might have come round and got out of his restraints, but who would he have called?

Communication in the oceans is not like in the cities. In those, you could tap a comm panel and get in touch with someone else's home easily enough. Many folks, those with more money than I had, had handheld devices that used the city-web signal. Between cities, the best method of communication was via fibre cable. I'd done a few jobs repairing the cables, but they'd been laid before I was born.

The ancients used radio and satellites, microwaves and sundry other technology I couldn't even begin to get my head around. I knew that the military were still working on some form of quantum entanglement communication. They'd had a few sets working during the latter days of the war, but I'd never heard if they rolled it out to the whole fleet. Cost was probably an issue.

Under the sea, radio is useless, lasers good for short range, and microwaves pointless. The satellites might still be in orbit, but that would mean breaking the surface and no one wanted to do that. The danger was too great. Skimmers revelled in it, the rest of us had sense.

You could use sound, like the great whales. That travelled for thousands of miles. Get the frequency correct, something very low. Send it down the DSC, Deep Sound Channel, a horizontal layer of water where the speed of sound was low, and someone would pick it up four, maybe five, thousand miles away. Whether that was the person you wanted to or not, you had no control over. The cities, and subs, sometimes used it to send out general messages, warnings, or maydays. It wasn't secure.

So, for a message to pop up on my sub, stolen sub, was unexpected.

The screen showed that a high powered laser communication had been initiated. A single word, "REPORT", on the screen in green. Below it, a cursor, a short line, flashed, awaiting my response.

"Bugger it."

"What is it?" Elena asked, as she slid into her seat beside me.

"Someone thinks Keller is on-board." I stared at the cursor. Whoever it was wanted a response.

"What are you going to do?"

Good question, what was I going to do? Lasers worked, if you knew where you were aiming and they clearly did, for about half a klick, five hundred meters. My hand hesitated over the keyboard.

"REPORT" appeared again on the screen.

"Well?" she said.

"Right," I answered and tapped out a response.

"Success? Is that all you are going to say?"

"What did you want me to say? 'Sorry, we killed your man and stole his sub. We are just heading home to report it to our military. You have a nice day.' I don't think that would go down well?"

"Well," she said, but didn't take the sentence any further as another message wrote itself upon the screen.

"PROBLEMS?"

"NONE." I sent the response and brought up the map of the area, such as it was. A top speed of 10 knots does not give you a lot of options for escape.

"There are a few canyons we can dive into," I said, more thinking out loud than expecting a response.

"Why don't we just make a run for it?"

"10 knots of running, in a worker sub designed to stay close to its home city, is unlikely to get us far. It is better to hide."

"DESTINATION?"

"What are you going to say?" she asked.

My hand hovered over the keyboard as I considered her question. I really had no good answer. A simple piece of logic suggested that this was not a random encounter. Whatever was out there had been heading towards Keller's mine and that meant they likely knew what was going on, or rather what should have gone on.

"I'm going to stall," I answered. I sent the sub into a shallow dive. Nothing quick, that might draw their attention. Just a slight change of course to put us near one of the canyons.

"DROP OFF." I messaged them back. The laser didn't bounce back which would have given me a range, but I could take a bearing and extrapolate the position of my follower. Somewhere behind and above. Not a lot to go on.

"REPEAT." Another fix. I am sure a brilliant physicist could have worked out how far away the message originator was by some change in the light. I am not a brilliant physicist, I had to guess.

"SORRY." It was as vague an answer as I could think of.

My sub kept its course, slowly descending towards a canyon the on-board map told me would be there. If the map was wrong then I was going to hit solid rock, very hard. The sub wouldn't, let me correct that, shouldn't rupture, but there would be damage.

"Check the passive SONAR. See if it can tell us what is following us," I told Elena.

"They might be friendly," she said.

"They sent us a message without introducing themselves and expected an answer. They know who they are, and they think they know who we are. I don't think they're friendly."

I wiped my palms on the jumpsuit and waited. Another message popped up on the screen. I ignored it. I had nothing left to say. The navigation screen, a kind of three dimensional representation of the seascape around the sub based on nothing but maps already on-board, showed the canyon approaching.

"Elena?"

"It is not showing much of anything. Biologics here and there, and a faint mechanical above us. Nothing is clear though."

"Send it through to the navigation screen. We are going to try and hide." I pushed the glide planes down further, increasing our rate of descent. At this point, my hands itched to send out a ping or two of active SONAR, just to test the map. It would have been the safe, normal thing to do. Therefore completely inappropriate for a sub trying to hide.

The screen lit up with a slew of colours, each indicating a different passive sonar contact. She was right, there were biologicals everywhere. We were in the ocean, there should be life everywhere and lots of it used sound to communicate. A flicked through the menus and I filtered most of them out.

Another message appeared on the screen. They were concerned about my course. I ignored it. I followed the laser back to its source and it did not indicate the mechanical above. Mechanicals were really engine, prop or other noise that wasn't naturally in the ocean. They could be anything man-made and, sometimes, sound tended to bounce around the ocean. It reflected off the layers where changes in water density, temperature and flow, divided the ocean into distinct strata.

Passive SONAR was good. The computer on the sub was not. It simply had not been built, modified or in any way designed to play games of hide and seek. The laser was telling me the sender was aft of our sub, the passive SONAR was pointing to a mechanical above us. One that was going faster than us.

There was a problem with passive SONAR. You were blind to everything behind you, your own engines made too much noise. On larger subs, and military ones, they solved this by trailing hydrophones and other devices that listened into this blind spot. Keller's sub did not have any of those.

Something above us, and something behind us. That was not good news. However, the canyon lip was coming up quickly now.

"Strap in and brace," I said. "We are going into the canyon. If we can find a good place, I'll back the sub up against a wall or into a cave. We'll see if we can hide out."

Little power, silence and making the sub seem like part of the rock formations was our best hope. It was a trick that lots of the creatures used to hunt other creatures in the ocean. Wait, save your energy, and let your meal come to you. You'd think them lazy, but there is as much energy used up in waiting, unmoving, as in chasing a meal through the water.

Two clicks told me she had fastened the safety belt. I gave a tight smile and gripped the controls, pushing them down a little further, taking the sub into the canyon.

It wasn't that there was any change in the light, there wasn't any light to change, but I knew the moment I was below the rim of the canyon walls. A change in the sound coming through the hull, differences in the way the water flowed over the hull, the feel of the controls under my hands. I kept diving.

"STOP." The message flicked up on the Comms screen. Then again. Insistent.

I didn't stop. Down and down, 10 knots of speed, full power from the engines and crossed fingers, toes and intestines. If the map was wrong, we were going to die.

The current changed. It pushed against the sub and the engines whined, rising in pitch. I fought the controls, pushing them up, down, left, right. Twisting them to yaw the little craft into the current. The Nav screen spun, colours blurred across the image, any detail lost.

"What is it?" Elena shouted above the engines. She had one hand on the arm rest of her chair and the other pressed against the roof of the cabin, trying to hold herself in the seat.

"A deep water current, I think." I wrenched the controls again, let some of the power bleed from the engine and the sub spun around. Elena screamed. Or it could have been me. I wasn't sure at that moment. These deep sea rivers of cold, dense, saline water moved at incredible speeds, compared to my sub, and there just wasn't the power to do much about it. We had a choice, continue to fight the good fight and die, or rise up, back into clearer water, and take the risk of the other sub.

Death or possible death? I'll take the possible over certain every time. I pulled back on the controls and fed power back into the engines, forcing the sub to ascend before we got dragged too far.

"We are putting out so much noise they will be waiting for us when we come out. Go and find a place to hide. If they capture us, they might believe me when I say I was the only one on board."

Elena nodded, unclipped her belt and stood.

Some seventh sense, warned me a moment before it happened and I pushed the controls with one hand, reaching out for her with the other. I was too late.

The sub clipped the canyon wall. The front robotic arm and its housing caught on an outcropping. The sub, the full 10 knots of power pushing it upwards, tipped up. The aft rising higher, pivoting around the caught arm. Elena fell. Her head left a bloody streak across the control panels.

I shoved the engines into to reverse, pulling the arm off the outcrop and letting the sub adopted a lazy turn in the now clear water.

Once my own belt was off, I grabbed Elena under her arms and pulled her into the small space behind the chairs. She was breathing, a good sign, but there was a lot of blood and I couldn't see the wound.

The field dressing, a bandage with a large absorbent pad, in the first aid kit contained the flow of blood. The coagulants in the cloth itself would help to slow it down further, reducing the amount of blood loss. However, she was out cold and needed treatment. That was something I just didn't have. Head wounds can look nasty and be a tiny cut that bleeds profusely. They can also look nasty and be nasty. This one seemed to fit into the latter category.

"STOP ENGINES." The message beeped on the Comms panel and I complied.

"TOWING."

There was a metallic clang on the hull. Our sub started to move again, upwards, without the engines doing any of the hard work. They were winching me in. That was a big sub up there.

"Elena, I don't know if you can hear me, but I you're hurt. Hopefully, the people on the sub will look after you. At least until they can get the answers they want." I patted her hand, an awkward gesture, and sighed.

All the evidence of two people, and there wasn't much, I cleared away as the towing continued. The first aid kit, I placed near her unmoving hand and tried to make it look as if she had treated herself before passing out. It wasn't perfect. I am not sure what it was. Better than nothing, I hoped.

Then I tried to find somewhere to hide away. Not easy in a tiny, two man, sub.

## CHAPTER TWENTY-EIGHT

Part of my military training, apart from the Fish-Suit, focused on survival techniques. Difficult when a ruptured suit or holed sub would kill you in seconds and, should you survive that, at the bottom of the sea there are limited ways to 'live off the land' so to speak. However, they did teach us to evade capture, to hide and, if needed, to escape. I wasn't good at it.

The biggest problem, for me at least, was breathing. Finding a place to hide, easy. But staying still and being quiet. Not my preferred way of being. During the drills, whenever I hid, anywhere, all I would hear was my own breathing and it always sounded loud. I could go a whole day, maybe more, without ever worrying about how loud my breathing was, without even hearing my own exhalations. I could go weeks without thinking about it, it just happened naturally. However, as soon as I would hide anywhere, all I could hear was my rasping, loud, echoing, cacophonous breathing.

The noise made me nervous and, as a result, it got worse. The more I would think about breathing in a slow, even measure, the louder it would get. I felt sure that the hunters would be closing in, just following the sound of my breathing. In the end, I had to move to a different spot. Usually, I'd be caught in one of these moves. No surprise that I almost failed that section of my training.

So, in this tiny sub, with limited places to avoid detection, the focus on each breath was total. A slow inhale, hold, absorb all the oxygen I could, and a careful exhale. That was the plan and all it accomplished was to make my ribs hurt and my head dizzy. I had to stay put. There was nowhere else to go.

Through the engine compartment door, I heard the

hatch open and the hollow ring of boots on the ladder. The heavy tread of two people echoed through the thin inner walls as they moved about the cabin. They began to talk.

"Is she dead?" said one voice, a deep tone with an accent I couldn't place.

Some clumping around, a moment of silence.

"No, Chief. Looks like she's taken a blow to the head. Bled a bit and tried to patch herself up. Head wounds always look worse than they are," said a second voice. Same accent but higher pitched. Probably younger or a woman, hard to be sure.

A clatter of plastic on the metal floor.

"It must have been quite a bash. She is completely out." The first voice again.

"I'll get a medic team down here. They can do a proper assessment and get her to the sick bay. Once they patch her up, we can get some answers," said the second voice.

"Do it," the first said. "While you're waiting, search the sub. I want to know what she was doing out there and where she was heading."

"Yes, Chief," the second said.

"I'll go and report. The captain will want to know as soon as possible." The sounds of someone climbing the ladder were followed by a muffled call for the medical team.

I was breathing hard. I didn't mean to. I wanted to be quiet, but my lungs were doing their own thing. Any moment now the person left behind was going to swing the door to the tiny engine compartment open and peek in.

There wasn't much room in here. It was really just the small reactor, which drove the engines, powered the life support and generally ensured the sub didn't sink. The computer core was here too, kept cool by all the pipes and tubes that kept the reactor temperature low. You could walk in, hunched over, and move around the reactor and pipes, but there wasn't much space to hide. The space I had found was uncomfortable, wedged in between some pipes, a deuterium tank and its tritium bed mate.

My legs were pressed up to my chest, which didn't help the breathing issue. A valve, or something else metallic, was digging in my back and the cold pipe above my head meant I couldn't turn my head much. I needed a drink. Several, in fact. I could almost see that little bottle that Devra had taken from me, almost taste it.

The door opened. I held my breath. I couldn't turn to look so I closed my eyes and focused on holding my breath. It was torture. More painful than the valve or the pipe. There were no other sounds but the soft susurration of the pipes, the gentle hum of the reactor, and the blood pounding in my ears.

I wanted to breathe. I needed fresh oxygen. In my favour were the years of training, diving and Fish-Suit operation. You'd be surprised how long you can hold your breath, if you have the right motivation and a little bit of knowledge. The little bit in question is, and it makes a lot of sense when you know it, if you hold your breath long enough to pass out from lack of oxygen, you will immediately start breathing. The upshot of this, and my training officer kept on about this kind of thing, was that you could push and push yourself, far past what you thought was possible, and be certain that your body would cope. Sure, it might knock you on your arse for the liberties you had taken with it, but when it was all said and done, it would be just fine, and so would you.

It didn't always work. I've lost friends who pushed it too far. I guess their bodies didn't like them too much. Mine loved me. It should, I fed it beer and whiskey most days. It should be desirously, drunkenly, happy.

The door finally shut. Just as well, the red and orange splotches that swam in my eyes were flashing out a Morse Code SOS. I sucked in a deep breath, not caring, for the moment, if the searcher heard me or not.

It took another three before the splotches receded and another few minutes before my head stopped spinning. The sound of blood, rushing through my arteries and veins, quietened enough to make out the sounds beyond the door. Multiple footsteps, grunts of efforts and what sounded like, through the muffling effect of metal, curses, the whine of an electrical motor and the creak of something.

All of this went on for a few minutes and was followed by the tread of two people ascending the ladder. There must still be one on-board. I could hear footsteps and the groan of the pilot's seat settling under a weight. The computer core's lights, next to me, started to flash.

I suppose it is one of those vagaries of science that the computer could, on the user's screen, feedback all sorts of information about how it was working and any faults, but we liked the actual thing to have lights that flashed. Engineers could probably tell you what each of the lights meant, or even have conversation with the lump of precious metals and whizzing electrons via those lights. To me, it meant that someone was using the sub's computer.

It took a minute or two, three additional bruises and a nasty knock on my decidedly un-funny bone that sent numbing tingles up and down my arm, to extricate myself from my cramped position behind the pipes. The computer was still flashing away to itself as I slid the door back and peeked into the cabin.

A dark smear of blood marked the spot where Elena had lain unconscious. Red footprints marched around the small cabin and, sat with his back to me, was a figure in the pilot's seat. I watched as the figure shook their head and heard the grunt of frustration. It was a sight and noise that made me smile.

Before I had scrunched myself into my engine room hideaway, I'd employed a simple delaying tactic on the sub's computer. A few swipes of the menu, a press here, a choice there and the computer readouts had changed into the most obscure language I could find. The symbols and letters weren't even in standard. They were a series of sweeping curves, dots, dashes, faded lines and bold splodges. I had no idea what any of it said and, by the reaction of the person in the seat, neither did they.

You could, if you knew how, reset the language by following the steps from memory. You'd have to have an amazing memory though. There was one other way and I'd guess the person tasked with digging through the records to find out where we were going wouldn't want to do it. If they did, everything they were searching for would be lost. You simply reset the computer back to its default. It wiped the memory and you lost everything. That didn't bother me, I'd bet it bothered them.

I slipped out of the engine room and debated climbing the ladder. That would put me in the big sub, amongst all the troops, soldiers or civilian operators. My guess, this was a military sub. There were civilian subs that plied the oceans, trading, communicating, travelling, but for one to chase us down and capture us? Military. Had to be.

What I needed was a way to move around the big vessel without attracting undue attention. To do that, I would need to look, and act, like one of them. What I needed was a uniform and I knew just where to get one. The engine room had a toolkit and I hefted the wrench. It felt heavy and that was good.

## CHAPTER TWENTY-NINE

The shoes chafed my heels, the arms were a little short and the waist was tight. I had to leave the trouser button undone and hope the shirt covered it enough to pass muster. The previous owner, now clad only in his underpants, I'd stuffed into the engine room and sealed the door. He wasn't getting out of there without some assistance.

Before I left, I spent a moment resetting the computer to its factory default. It would take an hour or two to cycle through the process. If anyone interrupted it, the whole computer would shut down, the data would be lost and the process would have to be restarted. Either way, there would be no data, no trace, and no way the sub was going anywhere for a while.

Outside my stolen sub, the business of our captors went on without interruption. The moon-pool we'd been docked in was one of three. The other two were occupied. Those subs were not the stubby, protrusion covered, robotic arm wielding worker sub that I'd arrived in. These were sleek, dark, torpedo shaped hulls with short wings, more properly planes but everyone called them wings, which controlled the ascent, descent and turn of the sub.

The presence of the single pilot combat subs confirmed my original guess, a military sub. The uniform had already pushed me further in that direction. Even though I couldn't read the name or insignia, there was something familiar about it.

I held the small computer pad in front of me like a shield and walked, as confidently as I could manage, towards the doors at the far end of the large dock. The other workers kept on about their tasks and didn't spare me a glance. I was just another worker doing their job. At least, that's what I hoped I looked like and not reminiscent of a man who'd just knocked one of their friend's unconscious and stolen his clothes.

The dock door was open and I passed into the sub proper. None of the signs were in standard and the script tickled something at the back of my mind. It was all straight lines, no curves. It didn't look to be so much written as carved. The bells were pealing in my brain, but my ears weren't listening. It would come to me at some point. If it was important, I'd prefer it to be sooner rather later.

There were some things that were standard on the sub. The colour coding on the walls, for instance. Long stripes that ran the length of the corridor to indicate the direction of essential services. Red for the command centre, orange for engineering, green for the medical bay and so on. I've no idea how it became the standard for all military subs, but it was and I was grateful. My second reason to be grateful was that, unlike many men, I wasn't colour-blind. The military had strange ideas sometimes.

I chose the indigo strip, noted the direction of arrows within it and smoothly altered my direction. The corridors themselves were narrow, enough for two abreast and no more. I passed by bunk rooms, a mess hall, four toilets, and a rec room before the stripe led me to the information centre.

These typically housed the computer core, the sensor equipment, readouts, maps, SONAR and other systems needed to keep the sub from crashing into other subs or mountains that rose from the sea floor. It was occupied.

Three soldiers, two men and a woman, sat at their consoles, tapping the keys, poking the screens and muttering to themselves. Each wore a headset and had a microphone boom in front of their mouths. There were five more consoles, all of them empty.

I walked into the room and headed to one of the free consoles. The soldiers didn't look around. They stayed focused on their tasks and I was able to slip into a seat behind them all.

The keyboard was covered in that same script, the one I couldn't read. The screen was the same. Luckily, the addition of icons made it easier to choose the correct programme. The navigation and maps were my first stop. I didn't need to be able to read the language to know what it said. I just didn't particularly like what it told me.

This sub was not alone. There were five others. One to either side, and three directly behind, following. It was a standard sailing pattern. The flankers were clear of this sub's noise and could stretch their sensors out to front, side and behind. Those behind were blind to most things apart from the sub in front, but that served to mask their presence from anyone seeking them. A tight beam laser or even, and more secure, an insulated wire carried all the information the following subs would need to maintain an overview of the situation.

The second piece of bad news, the destination of these military subs, Base 1. Given the destruction of the Silent City it was unlikely they were going there to offer their apologies. I took note of their ETA. At least the numbers were in standard, another thing to be grateful for.

I closed the map and picked the sub schematic, noting the layout. Engines at the back, docks at the front, bridge in the middle, protected by the rest of the hull. Weapon systems were located at the strategic points to give covering fire on all aspects. Torpedoes formed the main bulk of the offensive weaponry, supported by a large rail gun that only fired forwards and some close defence rail guns that would take out any enemy torpedoes or fighter-subs.

It was well armed. It was going towards my home Corporation. Elena was on-board. So was I. Decisions, decisions.

"Hello?" the accented voice said from my left.

Bugger. I tapped the keyboard, clearing the screen I had been looking at, giving myself a second to prepare before I turned to look.

"Hello." I smiled up at him, and up, and up. Good lord,

he was tall. Blond hair, blond beard, blue eyes, no smile.

"What are you doing?"

"Just checking something." I tried another smile and jiggled the pad I had brought in with me.

"I don't know you," he said.

"That's true." No point arguing. He didn't know me and I didn't know him. Any story I could come up with would be too easy to pick apart. If I let him do the talking, I couldn't say too much that would sound false. I watched him think for a few seconds. His mouth opened and closed a time or two.

"Why are you in here? You are not assigned to this station."

"Just checking some information about the sub we brought in," I said. It was a version of the truth. I waved the pad one more time.

With large hands, he reached out and took it from me. His eyes scanned the information on it, pressing his thick fingers to the screen a few times, swiping them back and forth, and flicking through the data.

"It says here," he began and pointed at the pad. I stood as he spoke and took the pad from his hands.

"Yes, interesting isn't it. Anyway, it has been good to meet you, but I have to report back."

The befuddlement was clear in his crystal eyes, as I took a slow, confident walk from the room. My hands were covered in sweat, but the firm grip on the pad covered up the trembles.

Five big, heavily armed subs were on their way to Base 1. They were not going on a friendly visit. I needed to do something to slow them down. Sabotage the engines? No, that would stop just this one. Invade the bridge? Unlikely to succeed on my own. Recruit others? Where from? Train this sub's weapons on the others? That plan had merit, though it was likely that the torpedoes had Friend or Foe systems built in. The close range rail guns might do some damage, cause some confusion. Maybe the city would hear the weapon fire and be forewarned.

I checked the wall stripes, turned away from the weapon systems and headed off down the corridor. The pad was a good prop and I kept my gaze upon it, shaking my head every so often.

## CHAPTER THIRTY

The hardest thing about the walk through the sub was not getting dragged into conversations or being given orders by the ranks above. In that regard, it was just like my military service. Everyone higher in rank used that as an excuse to avoid doing their own work and passed it on to you. The shit always rains down, we used to say. Here was no different. I waved the pad or pointed to it whenever someone tried to stop me.

The sub was big. The schematics I'd peeked at told me as much, but the reality was tiring on the legs. Walk, turn, check the stripes, walk, turn and more walking. Soldiers moved around on their own business. It was all surprisingly easy and I carried a strange sense of disappointment the whole way.

At the end of the anti-climactic journey, I entered a room with only one other occupant. A woman sat hunched over a keyboard and screen, typing away furiously. Above her, four screens showed a readout of systems, power flows and other bits of information that I couldn't understand. It was all labelled with that same script and, for a moment, I had a flash of memory.

A man, blond hair and beard, quaffing a large mug of foaming beer and grinning madly as half of it spilled off his chin and down the uniform he wore. The taste of the sweet mead in my own mouth and an answering smile. Before I was married, before Tyler was born. A time when I was in the military.

I paused in the doorway as the memory lost its blurry edges and came clear. The signing of the treaty and the party afterwards. I'd been part of the force that went along to protect the top echelons. My small group of Fish-Suit troops had been tasked with ensuring there were no surprises being planned by the then enemy. It had all gone smoothly, war is opportunity but it is also costly, and the treaty was signed.

The after-party was legendary. They could drink and back then I was not the hardened, alcohol dependent wreck I was today. I could recall the first bit of the evening, but everything after the third pint was blur. The morning after, she was tall, blond, with firm muscles everywhere and I have no idea what her name was. That was a long time ago.

I was on a VIKYN sub and, it seems, the treaty was over and done with.

There were other consoles, other screens and keyboards, but they all flashed a single cursor and a few demanding symbols. I took the guess that they were asking a user to login and I didn't have a passcode. What I needed was one that was already open and luckily, there was one. If only the current user would make herself absent from the station. However, she didn't look like she was going anywhere.

I could talk to her. Tell her that the captain wanted to see her. I could be pretty convincing at times though my lack of accent, language and knowledge would make that three times as difficult as I wanted it to be.

So, talk was out of the question which just left the other way. It was fast becoming my signature move. A few more times and I'd be teaching it during an unarmed combat class to new recruits. Before she could turn or register my presence, I curled one arm around her neck and up under her chin. With my other hand, I grabbed the choking arm and added its strength to the pressure. My arms cut off the supply of air and the blood flow from both her carotid arteries. By pulling her back in the chair at the same time, I took away her leverage to escape.

Without air, you can struggle for time. If you've trained in a Fish-Suit, you can struggle for quite some time. However, without blood to your brain a few seconds is all it takes to become unconscious. Keep it up for a few seconds more and that brief sleep can be extended by hours.

A few more seconds and you could kill someone. It was all in the timing. Too little and they'd wake up whilst you were about your business. Too much and you'd kill them. I've never considered myself a murderer and today wasn't the day to start. As soon as she stopped struggling, I bashed her head twice against the console. She'd have a headache when she woke up, but she would wake up.

I took her chair and let her sleep on the floor next to it. The screen was covered in those VIKYN symbols which I couldn't read. If I'd had in-eyes, like Derva or the Mayor, it would all be clear. It didn't matter, like the others it had icons I could use to navigate most of it. And, like everything else, it was colour coded. Green was good, yellow was a warning and red meant bloody hell something is going wrong or don't press that.

I flicked through the icons, getting a feel for their meaning and systems. What I wanted was something that would slow the subs down, make them stop, or cause them to emit noise that the city could pick up. I tried for all three.

This room had access to, and controlled, all the communications throughout this sub. It also maintained the thin wire that linked all the other subs together. A little mischief here should go a long way.

First job, disrupt the on-board communications. Make it so that workstation couldn't talk to workstation, that orders didn't make it to their intended recipient and confusion would reign. It was a simple task of changing the links around, rerouting the bridge to the kitchens, kitchen to engine room and so on. Dragging and dropping those multi-coloured lines from one place to another. I had no idea who I was making talk to who, it didn't matter.

Second, slow them down. I cut the internal links between the computer core and the reactor. This set alarms off all over the ship. Someone was shouting through the unconscious woman's headset. I'd no idea what they were saying. It sounded urgent.

Last job. I flicked the icon that disconnected, I hoped,

all the wire links. If the shouting had been loud before, the poor woman would be deafened by the volume now. All things considered, I did her favour by knocking her out, but I doubt she'd thank me.

The main lights went off and red lights took their place. Klaxons and alarms drowned out the headset. Time to go. I closed the door behind me and joined the military personnel scrambling to their posts.

I picked the stripe I wanted and rushed along with them. There was shouting and officers, I picked them out by their need to wave at everyone else with the pretence that they were in control, berating the troops at every turn. Every time someone waved at me, shouted at me or stood in my way, I raced past without acknowledging them.

## CHAPTER THIRTY-ONE

The medical bay bustled with doctors and attendants all locking down equipment, setting up triage tables. It was clear they had drilled for this. There was always the chance this could be real and, given the heightened confusion, red lighting, alarms and lack of orders from the bridge, I hoped many felt this was real.

"Get out of the way". One of the nurses shouted at me and I took a step to the side. He rushed past, arms full of bandage rolls.

I did my best to slip in-between them all and get a good look around. The screens, high up on the wall, showed the names of the current patients and their vital signs. At least, that is what they were supposed to do, but the lack of people on the beds made the screen useless.

Where was Elena? They must have brought her here. It was, according to the schematic I had seen a little while ago, the only medical facility on the sub. I grabbed a nearby nurse, stopping him in his tracks.

"Where is the woman they brought in earlier?" The noise and rushing about would, hopefully, cover my lack of accent. Still, I made my best stab at it. A theatrical agent would never be knocking on my door, fame as a clip-star would never be mine. I could live with that, if I lived through the next few hours and days.

"Woman?"

"Yes." I waved in the general direction of the beds and held up the computer pad as the reason to be here. "Head injury."

"Let me check." The nurse moved to a console, tapped the keys, shook his head and came back. "Minor wound, released and transferred."

"Transferred? To where?"

"It doesn't say." The nurse moved away before I could ask him for more information.

I was left standing in the middle of the rushing medics, wondering where to go next. Transferred? Where do you transfer someone to on a sub? Well, either to interrogate them and in the current confused state that was unlikely, which left the brig, if the sub had one. If it didn't then I really had no idea where to look. The idea of stopping everyone on the sub and asking them was ludicrous. However, the idea of leaving her on the sub was not one that filled me with joy either.

"You." The word was shouted above the noise of everyone else.

I turned towards the door and began to walk out of the room. No destination in mind, just the need to get out of here before someone gave me orders, or realised I didn't belong.

"Stop. You. Stop."

Just keep moving, I told myself. No need to stop. Get out in the corridor and merge with the rest of the crew. I wasn't as tall as most, nor did I have the beard that many seemed to wear. A day or two's stubble was most I could boast at the moment.

The heavy hand that landed on my shoulder stopped me dead.

"You were the one looking for the woman?"

I turned and gazed into the bright green eyes of a doctor. The white coat over the uniform was the biggest clue. I had to look up into those eyes and was beginning to get a crick in my neck. Why was everyone on this sub taller than me? It was giving me a complex.

"I am," and I paused for a moment as my brain searched for the correct title. I was outranked here. Actually, I had no rank on this sub, I wasn't supposed to be here, but I had to play the role if I wanted to get off of it alive, "Doctor."

"Do you know why the comms are down? I can't get hold of the bridge," she said, and there was a look of irritation in her eyes.

"I don't. I'm sorry."

She paused, looking me up and down. I fought the urge to tidy up my stolen uniform. It wasn't going to look any better on me that it did now and, right now, it looked like it didn't fit me. She shook her head.

"Go to the bridge and tell them that the medical bay is ready to receive casualties."

I nodded. "Yes, Doctor. Um, Doctor, do you know where they transferred the woman to, the one brought in earlier?"

"You have your orders." Her voice turned cold and the words were sharp.

"Yes, Doctor." I let my head hang low, avoiding her gaze. I should probably have saluted, but I didn't know how to. A meek stance was my best defence. I heard her give a snort of disgust and walk away.

### # # #

The docks were crammed with technicians and engineers. There were shouts, calls and orders. How anyone heard the order meant for them was beyond my comprehension. It wasn't total chaos, there was the hint of purposeful disorder about it.

The small attack subs were being geared up for battle. Figures swarmed over them, disconnecting hoses, connecting wires, testing and scanning. It was impossible to be sure if their pilots and weapon officers were aboard, just a safe bet that they were. If I wanted off of this sub, and I did, they were not the way.

The sub, Keller's sub, still at its dock. There was no-one working on it, fixing it, or do anything to it whatsoever. Once they opened the docking doors, those below the moon-pool, I might, might, be able to leave in that. There were some big 'ifs' in the way of that. If they didn't see me, if they didn't wonder why the engines were starting up, if they didn't notice the sub sink under the water level. All those ifs meant that it was not an option. No sub, military or civilian would ignore a sub leaving their ship without clearance.

Now, the Fish-Suit? That was an option. I could dive alongside one of the subs leaving or find an air-lock and slip out. Noticing a Fish-Suit, a device designed to be stealthy, was a lot more problematic than noticing a two-man sub.

There were some ifs attached to this method too. One, if I could get the Fish-Suit out of its hiding place on the sub. One-a, if it hadn't already been moved. The caveat occurred to me as I considered the plan. Two, if I could get the Fish-Suit to a place where I could put it on without attracting attention. That was a big one. I was moving a heavy, bulky bladder full of Oxyquid and the attached suit. Three, if I could slip into the moon-pool or out of an airlock without being shot by armed soldiers.

There was the possibility that they had a Fish-Suit user on the sub and I could steal theirs. It would mean leaving my own behind. Not something I wanted to do.

In my favour, the shouting and rushing about would provide my cover. If you can't hide, act confident. It would have to be one hell of an act.

With a deep breath, puffing out my chest, I strode forward, gaze straight ahead.

"I belong here. I have my orders." I kept repeating the mantra to myself as I walked.

Three soldiers and a technician rushed towards me when I was only five steps into my journey. Like all the others they were tall. They towered over me and I could see the determination on their faces. None of four were smiling and they were not slowing down. I tried to match their look, brow furrowed and the best snarl I could make curled upon my lips.

They closed in and my heart beat faster, my stomach turned somersaults. I stuffed my shaking hands into my pocket and carried on moving. If they were after me, there was nothing I could do. If they weren't, I didn't want anything to give me away. There was a sheen of sweat on my forehead.

Fifteen steps, ten, five, three, two, one. A nod and I was past them. Now the struggle was not to turn and check. The confident act was either going to work or it wasn't. I kept moving, never more aware of each stride, each step. Never thinking more about the act of walking and, therefore, making each step feel as natural as breathing water. Which, to be fair, I almost did every time I put that suit on. So at least there was a precedence.

No shouts followed. No sounds of running feet, and no alarms. The sub, my target, was just ahead.

Without a pause, I clambered on board and down the ladder into the sub. The blood had dried to a rust coloured stain and the engine compartment door was still closed. I hoped the guard I'd knocked out was still in there and that I wouldn't have to go in.

The pilot's chair was comfortable when I slipped into it. The guidance computer was off, the engine was cold and the rest of the basic systems were ticking over. The few buttons I pressed did nothing. I flicked through a few of the menus that still worked. There was little to work with. Someone had interrupted the restart and it would take hours to get it working again.

That meant that the sub I had come in on, with Elena, was not going to get me off the bigger sub. That left two options. First, stage a coup and take over control of the big sub and sail that home. It was a nice idea with just one or two slight flaws. Namely, I had no support on board, no weapons, no idea where the bridge was, no clue who was in control, and didn't have the three months to a year to carry out such an insurrection.

The second option had fewer flaws but a similar level of risk. Drag out the Fish-Suit, get it to an airlock, and get off the big sub. It would leave me in the middle of somewhere, hopefully not too far from Base 1 and a chance at rescue. It might leave in the middle of nowhere and with no chances. However, staying on this sub was not an option.

Elena was gone. Probably in their brig, being questioned or tortured for information. It wouldn't be long before she cracked, everyone does. I still wanted to rescue her, but I had a responsibility to my city. And to me.

## CHAPTER THIRTY-TWO

I was getting good at this. The trick was complete confidence and a pressurised look on your face. Walk like you meant it, let your features tell everyone you had a place to go and they were better off not distracting you from it.

In that manner, I managed to get hold of a four wheel flatbed trolley. It was normally used to move air cylinders and other heavy, hard to carry stuff about the dock. Someone had left it, out of the way, against a wall and without pause, like it had always been mine, I took it.

Dragging the Fish-Suit out of the small cargo hatch, the filled bladder dangling like a ball sack under the flaccid penis of the suit itself. It wasn't pretty. I didn't care. The too small uniform was lifting and pinching my undercarriage, and I was sweating.

The trolley was a life-saver, a back saver at least. What I needed now was a place to climb into the Fish-Suit, a few cables to top up the power, and a door to the outside. That meant an airlock. You'd be shocked by how few of them there are on a large sub. Each doorway, each break, however small, was a weakness. Either in the strength of the hull or acoustically. For that reason, big subs had as few as they could manage and it was one of those rare beasts I needed to find.

In fact, I needed a Goldilocks one - it couldn't be too close or too far away. Pushing a Fish-Suit through the sub was bound to get me noticed sooner or later. Similarly, slipping into the Fish-Suit couldn't be done in the view of everyone. It would spark a fair degree of interest.

I pushed the trolley along the docks, past the little subs and all the crew fixing them up, arming and fuelling them. The main doors would lead back into the sub and too many people. There was, however, another exit. One that I was sure would lead into the armoury or the fuel stores, maybe both.

The best hope was the weapon store because you had to get the weapons on board first of all. You could use the moon-pools, but that meant ferrying the weapons in by sub, a slow process. Much better to dock, run an extendable corridor out from your main city and trundle the weapons in that way. The airlock would, therefore, be quiet large, but it would have room to move, power interfaces and, most importantly, be right at the back of the store and only used when the sub was in the dock.

A few crew came out of the store, using a trolley just like mine, to cart boxes of munitions to the waiting subs. I couldn't read the labels, but the drawing on the side indicated they were for the rail guns. Heavy slugs of lead, depleted uranium or other esoteric metals. Close range weapons for the little subs or point defence for the bigger ones.

They gave me a funny look as they went by. I nodded and smiled in return. Once they had cleared the doorway, I moved in, pushing the trolley ahead of me. The store room was long and narrow with a low ceiling. To either side of the main alleyway, box upon box of ammunition was stacked floor to roof. More boxes of rail gun slugs, but also more specialised munitions. The self-guided mini-torpedoes that the small subs could carry two or three of, self-propelled bullets that the subs' cannons used and a variety of more specialised mines, some thermal, some kinetic, some sticky. The last were nasty. You never knew if one had hit you. They stuck to your sub and did a variety of things, cut their way in with lasers, timed detonators, or acted as beacons for larger torpedoes.

There were more crew in here, big lads one and all. Well, apart from the big ladies too. It was hot and it stank of sweat. How much would it have cost to give them a little air conditioning or, at least, an air freshener?

It took a little deft driving to get round all the muscle-bound dockers, lifters and carriers. It also took an effort of supreme will not to gag on the stench. At the end of the corridor, my target.

The controls were simple to operate. Even the military wouldn't change the multi-corporation agreement on health and safety protocols. Hence, all air locks were colour coded, used the same icons and operated the same way. A quick press of a few buttons and the inner door swung open. It was not a silent operation. Lights flashed, klaxons sounded, alarms rang. All perfectly normal by the standards of health and safety.

There was silence behind me, stunned silence, for about five seconds before the shouting began. I ignored it, pushed the trolley in and began the sequence to close the door.

"Hayes, stop right there," shouted a voice I recognised.

Running down the alleyway, Elena was waving her arms. She'd somehow broken free and needed me to get her off this enemy sub. A smile spread over my face and I reached for the controls again, to halt the door closing.

Which is when I noticed the uniform she was wearing, and all the armed troops behind her. My hand froze, finger outstretched towards the controls. The smile on my face melted and dribbled down my throat to sit heavy in my heart and stomach. She didn't look as though she was in trouble. She looked like she was in charge.

"Fuck," I swore and that was the least I wanted to say.

I watched her run towards me, her hand dip to the sidearm in the holster on her belt, the door still closing. Her hand rose, aiming the weapon at me, finger squeezing the trigger. A flash from the muzzle and the echo of a gunshot. The metallic spang of the projectile striking the airlock door as it finished closing. I waved at her.

Now, I had to be quick. The time for re-thinking, recriminations and revenge was later. Right now, I needed to get out. I took a screwdriver out of the uniform pockets and stabbed it into the control panel. It took three blows to get the cover off and then a moment to strip the wires from the buttons and cross them. Any commands sent to the door, requesting that it open, even in the politest of tones, would go round and round and round the door system until the end of time, or the power ran out. Health and safety strikes again, the door controls were on a separate circuit to the rest of the sub.

I started to climb into the Fish-Suit as Elena thumped against the vision panel in the airlock door. I could see that she was shouting something at me, but the door was too thick to let sound through. It was designed to keep the pressure of the ocean out, a little sound wave was no trouble.

The butt of her pistol hit the clear panel a few times before she gave up. Her last gesture, before stepping out of sight, consisted of just one finger that she indicated I should insert somewhere no finger was designed to go. I gave her a smile in return and carried on struggling into the suit.

"Hayes, stop what you are doing. There is no escape." Elena's voice sounded over the airlock speaker.

"You can't stop me." I carried on dressing.

"I can."

"Elena, if that's your real name, the airlock is out of your control. I know how these systems work."

"Hayes, I don't need the controls. I have something else. I can tell you what happened." The voice was tinny but insistent.

"I know what happened. You killed them all. You and Keller. Well, Keller's dead and Base 1 has a warning. Oh, and I am getting off this sub. Goodbye, Elena."

"Keller? You don't know anything, Hayes. But that's not what I have to tell you. That's not the information I have."

I paused and looked up the clear panel. She was there, a knowing smile on her face. Smug and in need of a solid punch. I don't hold, much, with hitting women, but this one had killed a lot of people. Some of whom might have been my friends, given time. She clearly thought she knew something. I shook my head and got back to dressing.

"I can tell you about Tyler," she said.

I stopped. Chilled. Cold. Frozen. Tyler, my child.

"What can you tell me?" I shuffled towards the door.

"I can tell you what happened on that day. All you have to do is come out of there. I can tell you everything." She smiled through the transparent panel.

"You don't know anything." And it was more than likely that she didn't. I'd never met her before a few days ago, certainly not years ago when Tyler died, was killed.

"I was in the city," she started to say and then health and safety started to work against me. The inner door was closed and that meant that the airlock could be flooded. Not a problem, that's what needed in order to open the outer door. What I didn't need was the whole process to begin before I had the suit on. But that's what it did.

# PART FIVE
# CHAPTER THIRTY-THREE

"Fuck, fuck, fuckity, fuck."

It didn't make the process of clipping myself into the Fish-Suit any faster, but the swearing was great for stress relief and the fast rising water was inducing a lot of that. I couldn't afford for any sea water to get into the suit and mix with the Oxyquid. The two just don't go together and inhaling a lungful of salt water was a sure way to drown.

Up and up the water came, past my calves and knees. I was ahead, just. I'd put this suit on more times than I could count, this should be easy. The danger of imminent drowning was, I admit, a bit of a new twist to the whole thing, but nothing I couldn't deal with.

Gagging on salt water, freezing liquid filling my lungs, the taste of it on my tongue, my life flickering before my eyes, the world going dark, my fingers as claws, scrabbling at the controls, the burning in my chest, the panic in my mind. Tyler.

"Bugger, bugger, buggery, bugger." I fumbled the waist clips as the water climbed up my thighs. A pause, a deep breath, who knew how many of those I had left, and on the third attempt I managed to close the clips. My arms, I stuffed down the sleeves, sealed the front and the neck ring as the sea water reached my chest. I was still winning. Go me.

The hood was fixed tight round my head as the water climbed further. The last piece was the helmet which I rammed down, over my head, and slotted the locking rim into the tracks, twisting to seal it. Ha! Now the water could rise all it wanted to and I wouldn't drown.

I gave Elena, who had reappeared at the door panel, a little wave. Her face twisted into a contortion of anger. The beauty of a few days ago gone.

Drowning was no longer a threat, suffocating was. The commands to re-fill the suit flashed up onto the visor and I used the controls in the gloves to OK them all without reading all the warnings. The liquid, cooled by the time away from my body, and from the heaters that normally kept it at an optimum temperature, flowed into the suit. And by flow, what I actually mean is jetted, sprayed, right into the back of my neck. It hurt and there was no escape.

In a reflection of the sea water, the Oxyquid, after it had poured down my back, rose past my ankles, calves, knees and kept on going. The air I needed to breathe was being pushed out of the suit, through the valves. A stream of bubbles passing before my visor. A dark, twisted sense of humour those designers had. You could actually watch your last breath disappear before your eyes.

Here it was, that time again, once done, never forgotten, and by most, never repeated. I sucked the gel down. It was cold. At another time, it might have been called refreshing. It wasn't now. The gag reflex cut in and I choked it down. You can't control a reflex. They come from that lizard part of your brain, the survival section, the bit that tells your body to do something to save its life. It bypasses your thoughts like it is hotwired to muscles, valves and other bits of anatomy. Once it starts, you can do your best to overcome it and that's what my training, all those years ago, was about.

I could breathe again. It was a strange type of breathing, but it meant I was alive and, with a strange kind of elation, another wave in Elena's direction seemed appropriate. So I gave her one. The flashing red lights told me the airlock was full of water.

It was also the moment that the sound from the first explosion propagated through the hull. Someone was shooting at us, them, the sub. Someone was shooting at the sub I was on. Elena turned away from the panel and started signalling to the people behind her.

The red light steadied and the outer door began to open. I used the suit thrusters to move towards it and, as soon as the gap was wide enough, slipped out, into the dark ocean.

I let the weight of the suit carry me down, away from the sub that was still powering forward. Another explosion and the concussion wave caught me, sent me spiralling. It was in that rolling over and over that I noticed the ocean wasn't as dark as I had presumed.

All around were the lights of small subs, large subs, the flashes of light that indicated the firing of rail guns and mini-torpedoes. There was a war going on, or a battle at least, and I was stuck in the middle of it. The one consolation, my warning had been heard. Base 1 was defending itself. They wouldn't be concerned about me. Didn't even know I was out here. Hell, they didn't even know that the Silent City had been destroyed, all those folks were dead, or who was attacking them.

I was on my own.

As always.

# CHAPTER THIRTY-FOUR

My solitude was not undisturbed.

The waves of sound were not just noise. Not in water, not in the ocean. They had real force and the closer you were to an explosion, the more likely it was your eardrums would burst, blood vessels would rupture or, and I'd heard of it happening more than once, your heart would stop. Funny ideas of mortality the designers had, they did at least consider that if you were to die whilst donning a Fish-Suit your ears would be the best protected bits. Perhaps they thought your body would be identified by your earprints.

Whatever it was they actually did, the suit protected your ears from sound waves. There was some sort of adaptive system that let most noises through, but dampened those that would harm your hearing. Ingenious stuff. And it meant that when the first large sub imploded, I felt it rather than heard it.

I saw it too. A sudden darkness, darker than the deepest trench, and then a cascade, a fountain, an eruption of air. Gigantic bubbles racing through the ocean being chased by smaller ones. The largest didn't make it far before imploding and forming millions of smaller bubbles. The other subs, the larger ones were rocked by the implosion, the smaller vessels were sent reeling through the ocean. I weighed much less than they did and was made to tumble, somersault and spin. The little thrusters gave up the battle pretty quickly and I tucked my arms in, clamped my legs together and tried to survive the ride.

Oxyquid cushioned my head. The exoskeleton hardened and the visor splashed up warning after warning. I couldn't read a single bloody one of them. The fact that they were red and flashing was enough.

Over and over, round and round, up, down, spin,

tumble, cartwheel, cavort, dance, jig. Pick your description. I closed my eyes and hoped.

When I'd slowed enough, the whine of the thrusters intruded on my thoughts of impending death. The Nav window was the first one back on line, sensors picking up the sound and electrical emissions from the vessels in combat, triangulating it with the magnetic field and its own active sonar.

My spin slowed, though my head kept going round at a thousand knots an hour. Dizzy, stomach fluttering and twisting, Oxyquid tasting of bile. I've never suffered from motion sickness, but right now I'd have killed for a scopolamine pill, or ten.

Active sonar? What the fuck. My suit had decided that, in the midst of a battle between five, now four, large subs and the outer defences of Base 1, it would be a good idea to make as much noise at it could. Send out a signal, again and again, that told everyone where I was. It was unlikely that any of the subs were searching for me in particular. The munitions whizzing round the battlescape, those that had lost their target, would find that signal and home in, sure of an easy kill. I flicked the controls in the gloves and shut down the active component.

It was too late. The Nav window showed a contact closing in. At this point, my instructor had told me, it was tempting to turn round and start blasting away, to take some aggressive action, to destroy your attacker. Well, he had said, good luck to you because all you'll have is your sidearm and that won't travel more than five feet in the water, and only if you throw it. I didn't even have that.

But, it was my suit, set up for me, and I knew how it worked. Two flicks, three screens and a deep breath. The suit went quiet. The heads up display went dark. The exo-ribs stopped helping and the joints relaxed. To all intents and purposes, the suit was dead. This is what the suit was designed to do, to be invisible and keep its user alive.

Swimming in a Fish-Suit is not easy. In that regard, they

are misnamed. It was the best I could do without the motors and I needed to be away from the last spot the contact had seen me at. The easiest direction was up. Natural buoyancy assisted and you could, therefore, rely just on your legs. Hold your arms by your side to maintain a streamlined shape and kick. I kicked like mad.

I heard the contact, by the noise and speed of passage, a small sub, pass underneath. The temptation to turn on the motors was great but resistible. I carried on kicking.

The battle went on around me. Lights still flashed in the darkness and concussion waves still battered the suit as I rose. I was going the wrong way. The best place for me was the sea bed, where I could hide amongst the rock formations, where I could skip from cover to cover. Where I could be ignored and make my escape.

It is reassuring to be in control again and the motors restarted without a qualm. I sighed. As much as I could sigh with lungs full of Oxyquid. Reversing my motion, the motors took me down towards the sea floor. The display flashed up, then died, and came back. All good, so far, but I was now relying on second hand information. Whatever noise, signals and signs the suit could pick up, process and deliver to my eyes. If there was something else out there being stealthy, I wouldn't see it. I'd also be a second or two behind reality. It took that long for the on-board computer to sort the confusion into information I could use.

### # # #

The motors pushed me down through the water column. Not fast or loud, but that suited me. The lack of noise was my best defence. The computer continued to try and make sense of the battle raging around me. It was struggling.

Big computers, those on large subs or in cities, found tracking the complex sounds of battles difficult. Many times, and certainly during the wars, attack groups had planned their runs beforehand and stuck to the plan, the courses, the speeds and firing solutions, above everything else. Those commanders who decided to deviate from the plans all too often caused chaos.

The thing is, battles do not follow the plans laid down by commanders. Things change quickly, the situation is fluid. I didn't have much of a plan, I was free to adapt.

It came from nowhere and there was no chance to get out of the way. A thin fighter, engine pods on the side, torpedoes to either side of the canopy. A single pilot who looked as shocked as I did when the sub caught me square in the stomach and I folded over it. The visor of my Fish-Suit bounced off the pilot's cockpit. He didn't look very old, just scared.

He pulled back on the controls, more in reflex than anything else and up we went. His sub was faster than my suit so I slapped my left hand down onto the hull and engaged the magnets. There was a solid clank that ran up my arm, through my neck and into my skull, as the glove secured the contact. Now that I had him, what was I going to do with him? The temptation to wave was strong.

The pilot, shock wearing off, flipped the stick, sending the little sub into a roll. Compared the last time I was sent spinning, just a little while ago, this was nothing. The glove was not going to let go and I pushed some power to the elbow joint just to make sure it was stiff enough not to break my arm. And then back the other way, and I was so glad I'd shoved a little extra into the shoulder joint too.

When it was clear I wasn't going anywhere, he levelled off. It had to be clear to him that I was no threat and that there were bigger fish in the sea to worry about. I had no idea what side he was on. Mind you, he didn't know who I was.

He kept it level for a moment as he checked his screens. It was almost possible to see the thought patterns go round in his head. He had a man stuck to his sub, increasing his noise presence in the ocean, and he had a battle to survive. He could pilot with just the sensors and screens, that's what most did. Past a hundred meters down there was no light anyway, except that which the subs brought with them.

His mistake was thinking I was no threat. It took me a moment to realise I could be. I gestured to him, getting his attention, and indicating that I was going to shift around, move into a position that brought some streamlining back to his sub. The pilot shook his head, in frustration I guessed, rather than telling me not. He didn't have any choices.

By reducing the power in the glove magnet I could stay attached and slide around the small sub. All the while, he did his best to ignore me. He was focused on his screens, managing his power levels, noise, his sonar, engines and everything else. Being in control of a combat sub during a battle was difficult and confusing. My Fish-Suit was difficult to use, but compared to a combat sub it was an abacus. I shifted the beads along the wires in two dimensions, he moved the beads between wires in four or five.

As I moved, I sought out the bit of the sub I wanted. It would be near the canopy, just below it in fact. The glow from his canopy, low and subtle, was enough to illuminate my target. A small latch, a handle really, surrounded by warning signs. One quick tug on the handle and the canopy would pop open. Sadly, for the pilot inside, death would painful, but quick.

Before I could carry out my plan, the torpedo next to me started spinning up. The small propeller at the rear of the long, thin bomb whirred. I felt, rather than heard, the two clicks as the clasps let go of the weapon which sped off into the dark. I couldn't pick the resulting explosion, if there was one, from the rest of the noise. My suit sensors tracked the torpedo into the confusion, but even it could not tell me whether it hit its target. Or even what its target was.

I gave the handle a pull. It rose out of its housing and then stopped. The canopy stayed closed. I tried again and again. It still did not open. Inside the cockpit, the pilot turned to face me, a look of fear and panic clear on his face. His hands flew over the keyboard, tapping at the keys with a speed that should have been impossible, searching through menus. Now that I could make out the language on his screens, I didn't feel so bad about killing him. I couldn't read a word of it.

The handle wouldn't budge on the next try or the one after. A single raised finger from the pilot indicated he had managed to lock me out. Opening the hatch whilst the sub was in the water and in motion was not advisable. Health and safety should have come to rescue once again. The general protocols insisted that a canopy could be opened by someone outside, in case of an accident and the need to recover the pilot.

What he had done, was to override the hatch control and lock me out. That was fine. I had my own key. A few taps on the fingertip controls in the gloves and, on the top of my free hand, the mini-cutter sparked to life. The batteries would drain quickly, but long before they ran out I intended to be sat in his seat and piloting his sub back to Base 1.

My visor darkened, protecting my eyes from the blistering blue white glare of the cutting flame. I pushed the hot blade into the hatch and started to move it left, then down, back to the right and up again. All the while, the pilot, oblivious of the threat and secure in the knowledge that I was a mere remora to his shark, kept the sub moving through the battle space. Twisting, turning, rolling, yawing, and every other move that his instructors had taught him. What he was dodging or trying to get behind, I had no idea. I didn't see, couldn't see, a thing.

There was a pop and hiss of escaping air as the metal surrounding the hatch came away and the air within escaped. With access to the mechanism and wires inside it was the work of a moment to open the canopy.

## CHAPTER THIRTY-FIVE

Another death to add to my tally. This one was as pretty as the last, as Keller's. I did feel a little guilt this time. The pilot hadn't done much to me, but his corporation had. It had killed everyone in the Silent City and had tried to kill me.

There was a moment of fear on his face. Just a flash before it was replaced by pain and terror. I knew what happened to the human body at the bottom of the ocean, under pressure. I'd seen my crew die in just such a way and been unable to do anything about it. The memory made me realise I hadn't had a drink in a while. I needed one now.

Dark, cold, salt water would have rushed up his nose and forced its way into his mouth. A single, tiny gap would be all it would take for the water to find its way in. The air being crushed out of lungs by the pressure of the ocean would create that opening. All that liquid would fill his lungs. I could empathise with him, it's what I did whenever I put this suit on.

He was drowning, but it got worse. The sea water, under all the pressure from the water above, would invade any orifice. It would have forced its way into his ears and, as a result, burst his eardrums. With the way open, the water would have pushed further into skull.

The water would have forced its way up his nostrils and then down his throat, overcoming the muscles designed to prevent drowning, the ones that reflex controls. The headache must have been incredible, but he couldn't scream. You need air to scream. All he had was water.

Mercifully, it didn't take long for him to lose consciousness and, once he stopped twitching, I released him from his chair, pulling him from the sub. His body fell behind the moving sub as I settled into his seat.

The controls and screens still worked. You didn't build

a vessel designed to work under, and surrounded, by water that would break down when a little bit got into the cockpit. The writing, labels and anything I actually wanted to read were in the language I couldn't understand. That was fine. All I wanted to know was the location of the large sub that Elena was on and how many torpedoes I had left.

The Nav screen, cross linked with the sonar, suggested a large contact some distance away and, apparently, moving away from the battle space. A quick visual check showed one torpedo left on the sub.

A push on the rudder pedal and my new sub started to turn towards the marker on the screen. In my hand, the joystick shook a little, no doubt resulting from the absence of a canopy. I pulled back a little and sped up the turn, raising the nose and pointing it towards my target. The throttle, I pushed forward to its maximum speed. This was dangerous. Added speed meant more motor noise, more noise from the propeller, more noise from the rattling and shaking of the damaged sub.

I kept my eyes glued to the Nav and sonar screen. The fire control, the trigger, below the first finger of my right hand would only take a little squeeze to arm and send the torpedo on its way. My thumb, on the top of the joystick, had access to the counter-measures, really just simple canisters that were shot away from the sub and made a lot of noise. The aim was to confuse any sonar locks of enemy vessels or, worse, their torpedoes.

Red flashes on the screen indicated that other contacts were closing on my sub. I was probably the noisiest thing in the ocean bar a passing whale in heat. In the ocean you are either silent or very loud, there is no middle ground, and though my training cried out for stealth, I went with cacophony.

One, two, three, canisters flew off from the sub. Immediately, they began to spin, to emanate low frequency and high frequency noise, gas under immense pressure was released in a continuous stream of bubbles, mimicking the cavitation of the propeller. I kept my course true and ignored the incoming contacts.

Gauging the sonar readings, I was coming up behind my target. Its propellers would mask my approach, but the noise from my attackers might alert them to something. Every ten or so seconds, I fired off another canister. Hiding myself in the confusion of noise.

A concussive wave hit my sub. The Oxyquid did its job and cushioned the blow, but the near miss sent my sub into a spin. I fought with the controls, righting the sub and setting it back on course.

Within a minute, maybe less, my torpedo would be in range. I sucked in a deep lungful of life preserving liquid and focused my gaze on the screen, firing off another canister. Just in case.

The contact grew larger on the screen. As did a collection of new ones, closing in from either side. I pushed the throttle as hard as I could, dragging every knot possible from the little sub's engines. The whine behind me increased and red lights began to flash on the console.

I kept going, employing tiny adjustments to ensure I stayed on an intercept course. All around the little gold triangle that represented my sub on the screen, the red dots that indicated all the other contacts were starting to crowd the screen. At least that portion of it that surrounded me. My target, the largest contact, was almost in firing range.

One torpedo, especially a little one like the one on this sub, wouldn't be enough to destroy Elena's sub. I knew that. It might be enough to slow it down though, to disable it a little and give me the chance to do something else. During the war, people feared Fish-Suit troops. Maybe it was time they did again.

Her sub was finally in range. Revenge tasted, well it tasted of Oxyquid at the moment, but once I was back home it would taste of beer and whiskey. I needed a drink now. A first squeeze of the trigger and the torpedo next to me began to spin up, locking on to large submarine. The screen flashed as the contacts around me multiplied. They'd clearly determined I was threat and had fired their own torpedoes, hoping to head off my attack.

I thumbed off two more canisters from my dwindling supply and continued to hold down the trigger. Hopefully the countermeasures would distract a few, if it not most, of the torpedoes heading my way. There was jolt from the left side of my sub as the torpedo launched.

The screen showed it heading fast and true. I could afford a smile, so I did, and slid my thumb across the top of the joystick to press down on the defensive rail guns. The first set of explosions struck my sub. The little craft bucked, reeled, and the joystick in my hand was wrenched to the left and right.

There was a further series of explosions, a chattering from the rail guns on my sub, and the whine from my engines reached a frequency way above human hearing. The console's screens flickered, went off and then came back on. Now though, all the contacts came accompanied by two or three ghost images. In the mix and confusion of images, my own torpedo appeared to be heading true to course.

Sadly, the same could not be said for my own submarine. Without understanding the language, there was no way to accurately gauge the actual level of damage the vessel had suffered.

My best guess, the engine was about to die. I couldn't hear it any longer and my speed, even with the throttle pushed far forward, was less than my suit could achieve. I had no large weapons left. The canopy was gone, but I did that. The computer was having trouble, the ghosts on the screen just a symptom. Add to that, the stick controls didn't seem to be doing much.

Time to go. I fired off the last of the canisters, at least they still worked, and wormed my way out of the pilot's seat. A kick from my suit engines lifted me clear and I pushed them hard to carry me away from the doomed sub.

There was another explosion and the concussion wave

picked me up, throwing me further from the disintegrating sub. It was followed by another wave, a smaller one, and all I could hope was that it marked the impact of my own torpedo.

With nothing else to do, no other threat to offer, and enough battery power to get me back to Base 1, I let the suit carry me down to the sea floor and started walking. It was quieter that way. Using the motors only to clear the obstacles I couldn't climb or swim over, no need to draw the attention of the combatants above.

## CHAPTER THIRTY-SIX

The cell was nice. I'd been in worse. This one had a comfortable bed, an entertainment screen and they brought me regular meals. There were a couple of downsides. I wasn't free to leave and they wouldn't serve me any alcohol.

The guards were friendly, if you discounted the charge-batons they held and the weapons holstered at their waist. Their conversation wasn't up to much, but they didn't go in for the random beatings and senseless violence that some others I'd known enjoyed. All in all, it was better than my apartment.

The soldiers from Base 1 had picked me up in one of the city's moon-pools. I'd surfaced to see a multitude of rifle muzzles pointed at my helmeted head. Instructions appeared on my visor and I followed them to the letter. The threat of death by firing squad was a powerful motivator.

A crane had lifted me, suit and all, from the pool and deposited me on the dockside. The muzzles tracked the whole process. A few more instructions followed and I keyed the commands into the suit. Oxyquid poured out as the seals released. A helpful soldier stood to one side to receive the helmet, which I dutifully placed in his hands.

The usual coughing, vomiting and retching followed. My lungs forcing all the liquid out of them and replacing it with city air. Sometimes they tried to do both at once. This brought on the really big fits of heaving. At this point, having seen a man go through something like this, you'd have thought that someone would have offered me a drink or, at least, a cloth. Nope. No such humanity for me.

The sergeant in charge didn't speak except to give instructions. These he barked at me in a staccato barrage of words. The basics seemed to be, don't talk, don't speak, don't move unless told to, don't raise your hands, don't move your hands, do as you are told when you are told. If I didn't follow these instructions I would be shot and a note of condolence would be sent to my next of kin if there was enough of me left to make identification.

I took him at his word and, in the knowledge that there were rather a lot of weapons pointed in my direction, and complied with everything. Firstly, strip down to my underwear. Not a problem, apart from the suit all I had on was the Fish-Suit underwear. I'd been wearing them a few days.

Second, the march down the corridor covered in the sheen of gel. Surrounded by soldiers, I was shielded from the view of the inhabitants of Base 1. It was probably more for their benefit than mine.

The third instruction was simplicity itself. Sit in the cell and don't cause any problems for the guards. They let me have a shower, though they did steal my clothes. I never got to see those again. To be fair to the hospitality, they did provide me with a rather fetching bright yellow jumpsuit and some underwear that was only a little too big.

Two days later, I was still there. The guard, a man whose name I had yet to learn and they had no name strips on their uniforms to inform me, slipped the tray full of food through the slot at the bottom of the door and bashed his baton on the door itself to let me know his time training as a waiter wasn't wasted.

I was tucking into the fish stew and glass of water they'd thoughtfully provided when a shout came from behind the door.

"Put your hands on the back wall, your legs apart and do not attempt to move. If you do, you will be shot."

Facing the wall, there was no way I could see them enter. The multiple sets of footsteps were a clue that there was more than one as was the second voice, which spoke next.

"Put your hands behind your back," it said.

The handcuffs snapped into place with professional speed, ease and a decidedly final sounding click. A hand grabbed the cuffs and pulled my arms up, high behind my back, forcing my head into the wall.

"You will not struggle. You will do as you are told. You will not speak unless asked to. Is that clear?"

I grunted in response and received a hard slap on the side of my head.

"Yes, that's clear," I said.

"Take him to room 3, sit him down and hook him up," said the first voice.

"Yes, sir," said the second.

My arms were lowered, hands grabbed my elbows and guided me from the cell. There was a soldier either side of me, both holding charge-batons in their free hand. I could hear more footsteps behind, probably the owners of the first and second voices.

The room they led me to, room 3 apparently, contained a chair attached to a plinth, a small cabinet on wheels with a screen on top, and a table with two chairs next to it.

It wasn't a complete shock when they released my cuffs and strapped me into the chair. The guards backed away and another man approached. He began to draw cables from the box and attaching them to my fingers, toes, and ear lobes. There was also a strap that encircled my forehead from which a cable dangled. The end of this cable went, like all the others, into the box.

Once he had done his job, the man backed away to stand on the opposite side of the box, turning the screen to face him. At that moment, another man walked in, nodded his approval at the scene in front of him, and sat in one of the chairs at the table. I saw him take a pad out of his pocket, place it flat on the table and begin to scan through the various screens. After a time of watching, I got bored.

"Hi," I said.

One of the guards shifted forward and raised the charge baton to strike me. The man waved him away.

"Hello, Mr Hayes," he said and turned out to be the owner of the first voice. His hair was grey, cut short, and there were lines around his eyes. The way he sat, and the way he had come in, suggested he kept himself fit and active.

"Why am I here?"

"It is an interesting approach, to ask questions of your interrogator," he said. "Has it ever worked for you?"

"Always a first time," I said and turned my head to the side to see what the man with the box was doing.

"It is ready," that man said, proving out to be the owner of the second voice. He had a friendly looking face, young without being too young, with a light stubble on his chin, probably just to prove he could grow some facial hair.

"Good. Now, Mr Hayes," the first man said, "this will go a lot easier for us all if you just answer the questions simply. We'll start with some yes/no questions and I'll ask for any details I want. Don't think you are being helpful by volunteering information I don't want. It will just slow us down and I haven't slept for two days. I get grouchy when I don't sleep and we have ways of... encouraging... you to be truthful."

There was a high pitched whine from the box next to me and I imagined the electric shock running up the wires. Perhaps I was just lucky they hadn't attached any to my balls. Or maybe that was for later on.

"Fine," I said, and tried to smile. "Ask away."

I really hoped I had nothing to hide. I didn't think I did, but sometimes you never knew. The police have been known to make things up and these guys weren't the police. They were something worse. I'm pretty sure the fellow sat at the table was a lawyer.

## CHAPTER THIRTY-SEVEN

"Your name is Corin Hayes?"

"So my mother told me," I answered and the noise emanating from the box rose further in pitch.

"If you don't get the hang of this quite quickly, Mr Hayes, I can promise you, it will hurt," the man sat at the table said in a reasonable, calm, voice.

"Is your name Corin Hayes?"

"Yes," I said, and the pitch lowered a little.

"See. That was easy wasn't it?" He smiled at me like a parent whose child has just learned to tie their laces. "You were a member of a special forces unit?"

"Yes."

"Good, very good. You were contracted to repair the scientific outpost?"

"Yes."

He flicked through a few more screens on his pad, nodding and tapping the screen as he went.

"I see your child was murdered."

I didn't answer. It wasn't a question and I didn't want to go there. Not here. Not in these circumstances. The man looked up when I was silent. He gave me a look, one I couldn't read and then cast his glance to second man who nodded in response.

"Do you know what work the scientific outpost was doing?"

"Not really." I shook my head. It was the truth, I hadn't had time to find out.

"Do you know who owned the submarines that attacked this base?"

"VIKYN."

He tapped at the pad a few times. "And how do you know that?"

"I was on-board one of their subs. I saw the language and insignia."

"Are you now a member of their corporation, or have you ever been?" he asked.

"No."

"Interesting," he said.

I stayed silent, it wasn't a question and I'm adverse to pain. He kept scanning the notes on his pad. Tapping the screen here and there, swiping his fingers across it.

"Why were you on the sub?"

"They captured me as I was making the journey from Calhoun to here."

The first man looked up and gestured to the second man who, in turn, made a gesture to the two guards. Without a word the guards left the room, closing the door firmly behind them.

"Did you cause the destruction of that city?" he asked and leaned forward over the desk.

"No." I had to take a deep breath before I answered.

The first man looked at the second who, I noted, nodded.

"Do you know who caused the destruction of the city?"

"Yes."

"Well?" he prompted.

"A man called Keller, he was the foreman, and a woman named Elena. Their names and details should be on file. They had both been there for some time," I explained.

"Tell me what happened."

I began at the beginning and tried to describe everything that had happened since I docked at Calhoun. Some bits, I may have left out, none of it important. I talked about my dislike for Keller, the argument we had, the moment I caught him tampering with my Fish-Suit.

When I spoke of the rest of the crew it was with a note of sadness in my voice. They'd made me feel welcome and for the first time in a long while I was back in the fold. I was back with friends, with colleagues, people with whom I could share experiences. It hadn't lasted.

"What about Elena?" he asked of me.

"She was in it with Keller. I didn't think she was at the start," and to be honest up until I had seen her in that uniform I hadn't even thought about the possibility, "but it became clear that she was. I should have put it together sooner. She was in the base and I assumed that Keller had kidnapped her."

"And you rescued her?"

"Well, yes," I said. "I didn't know she was one of them did I?"

"And you wanted to have sex with her?"

"The thought had crossed my mind, but more than that she was in need. She had been kidnapped. Seen all her friends die and I thought Keller was going to rape her. It seemed a good idea to get her away."

"What about Keller?"

"He's dead." I couldn't keep the anger from my voice and saw no pressing need to.

"You killed him?" he asked.

"I didn't see him die, but there was no way he could have survived the steam and what it did to his face." I knew there was a smile on my face, a pride in the revenge I took, and I knew that it was wrong.

"His face?"

"I blasted his face with superheated steam. It cooked him in a flash. Even his own mother wouldn't have recognised him."

"So, and just to be clear, you can't be sure it was Keller?" the first man asked and waved a hand at the second. The box whined and the first man spoke again. "Think carefully about your answer."

I did think and then I spoke. "I did not see his face before the steam hit. I could not recognise him afterwards. I am assuming it was him because he brought Elena and me onto the base."

"But he didn't know you were attached to the sub, did

he?"

"Of course not. If he had, he would have killed me in the water or when I was climbing out of the pool," I replied.

"And you didn't see him in the base?"

"Until he was on the floor with a face like boiled maggots? No, I didn't see him." What I did have was a bad feeling about the direction this interview was going. "Are you telling me he isn't dead?"

"I'm not telling you anything, you are telling me the things I want to know. I thought I had made that clear at the beginning of this interrogation." He stood up from his chair and moved around the table to stand in front of me.

"He is not dead is he? Damn it all to fuck. At least I got Elena." Though there was small hope of that. The small torpedo would do little damage to a large sub. I had been behind it, aiming at the drive, trying to slow it down. So maybe, perhaps, if I'd got lucky, the torpedo would have disabled her sub for someone else to pick off. "I didn't get her either, did I?"

He stared at me and I stared back, trying to read the truth in his eyes, his expression, and the way he stood. All I learned was to never play poker against him.

"What did you do on the VIKYN submarine?" he asked me.

"I tried to find Elena, before I knew she was working for the other side, and then I tried to disable it, and send a warning," I answered.

"And then?"

"Then I escaped."

At that he turned away and paced back behind his desk to sit down scan the pad.

"Keller was one of ours," he said eventually.

Hell.

"Well, I am sorry about that." I tried to sound sympathetic, but that man had killed a whole base. My sympathy was in short supply and I wasn't going to waste it.

"As are his wife and children," the first man said. "You

will be escorted back to your cell. I may have more questions for you later."

"I think not, Colonel."

All three of us turned to look at the doorway. I hadn't heard it open, but there stood another man I did not recognise. He was dressed in an expensive suit, clean shaven, hair perfectly styled and a superior smile on his face. Definitely a lawyer.

"Who are you?" the first man, now known as Colonel asked.

"I could tell you that, but then you'd have to be killed or at the very least posted somewhere unpleasant from where you would not return." The man in the doorway took a few steps into the room, letting the door close behind him. "It is safer, for you, to read the orders that were just transmitted to your pad and comply as promptly as possible."

The colonel looked the newcomer up and down, glanced at the second man, then at me, before looking down at his pad. I watched the emotions play across his expression as he read. From anger, to fury, to impotence and back to anger again. His face reddened and his hands formed fists on the table as he finished reading.

"Captain," the Colonel said without looking up, "disconnect Mr Hayes from the machine and release him from his restraints."

"Sir?" the second man, the Captain, said.

"Do as you are ordered, Captain, then clear the room, we are leaving the city."

"Excellent news, Colonel," said the stranger.

"You haven't heard the last of this," the colonel said. He stood and snatched his pad from the desk, stuffing it into his jacket.

"I look forward to filing your formal complaint. You can be sure it will be given all the respect it is due, Colonel. I believe bin collections are on a Tuesday." The suited man gave the colonel a smile so sincere that it passed through twelve dimensions of reality and came out the other side as anything but.

The Colonel waved the comment away and moved to leave. He stopped, turned and said, "Mr Hayes, this isn't over between us either."

"Of course not, Colonel." I smiled at him as I rubbed the life back into my hands. It has to be said, I had no wish to ever see the man again.

There was silence as the captain gathered up his machine and left the room in the colonel's company.

"I suppose I should thank you," I said to the man who had rescued me.

"I wouldn't go counting your seahorses before they hatch," he replied. "How do you know I did not release you from the clutches of military intelligence, the company's biggest oxymoron, only to have you at my mercy?"

"Did you?"

"Not yet." He smiled again.

"Who are you?"

"I could tell you, but, well you know the answer by now. Let's just assume I represent some important people and organisations within the company that have an interest in your well-being and having a clear account of events at the scientific base," he said.

"You're going to interrogate me now?" Frying pan and a rather large, hot, roaring fire sprang to mind.

"Interrogate no? I am going to feed you, let you bathe, have a drink and then we'll have a chat about the events. After that, I'll put you on the next transport back to your home city."

"A drink?" And suddenly the day had just got a whole lot brighter.

"Of course and before we start, I should probably tell you that the interests I represent have been back to the site of the outpost. We've recovered several bodies. Keller's included."

The day darkened again, a massive algae bloom blocking out the sun's rays.

"Keller wasn't on the Sub?" I asked

"He wasn't on the sub," he said.

"He didn't destroy the city?"

"He didn't."

"Elena did?"

"Well now, that is one of the things we need to discuss." He put a friendly hand on my shoulder. "Shall we go?"

# CHAPTER THIRTY-EIGHT

The beer sat untouched on the glass table top. The whiskey glass next to it contained a fair measure of amber liquid.

Silence encompassed the room. The subtle links of solitude and loneliness joined us together. Tom tended the bar and the jukebox hung on the wall, daring us to insert a coin and choose a song.

Everything was as it had been. Apart from the fellow I had found in my seat. I hadn't been gone that long, though I knew the rules. Dead man's shoes. Sadly, for him at least, this dead man was still walking and still had his shoes on. It had taken five minutes of mute staring before he'd picked up his own drink and moved to the empty table by the door.

My seat, my home. My place in the world. Days of memories to process and years of memories to let back in. I leaned back, let my head rest on the back of the seat and closed my eyes. Let them come, I thought.

And they did. Every face of every person who'd died, those I'd killed, those I'd seen killed and those I had found. The catalogue of faces was getting longer. Many I could put names to, but too many were without even that simple memorial.

Keller's was there and I offered his spirit an apology for thinking wrong of him.

The man who I'd steamed to death? Perhaps he'd been coming to release me, to feed me, or to just do his job and carry on with his life. It had been a horrible, painful way to go. I could spare a little sympathy, even in the knowledge that he was more likely to be a member of the VIKYN team who'd killed the rest. Or he could have been the janitor. I'll never know.

The faces kept coming, one after the other until, finally, and with a great sigh, Tyler's appeared. The smile, the hair, the laughs, frowns and tears. Tyler's face was the only one that moved in my memory, the one that I could see at different ages.

Her smile died. In the end, the last time, she didn't look like herself at all. Skin sagged around the bones on her face. Hair hung limp. The coroner had done his best to hide the bruises, but the cuts were impossible to cover up. Her eyes were closed and her chest was still. She didn't look peaceful, she didn't look like anything she had been in life. In that shell, that cracked and broken body, everything that Tyler had been was gone. Flesh, bone, organs, meat and gristle, that's all that lay on the slab. Empty. Like me.

"Fuck," I muttered as the tears came.

I picked up the whiskey and knocked it back in one big gulp. The fire burned down my throat, its heat adding to the rage already churning in my stomach. With the back of my hand, I wiped the tears away.

As I did, my gaze travelled up a pair of long shapely legs, across a flat stomach, small breasts and, at last, to Derva's beautiful face.

"Mind if I sit?" she asked.

"I don't think I could stop you, could I?"

She sat down, placing her own drink on the table top.

"You didn't come and see me when you got back," she said. It was a half accusation, half worry, kind of statement.

"I didn't want to see anyone. Which is pretty easy in my case."

"You know you've been cleared of all wrong doing?" Her eyes looked up from the table and met mine. "It wasn't your fault. The mayor feels terrible for sending you into that. It was supposed to be a simple repair job."

"It was sabotage. VIKYN destroyed that city. There were explosives on the support struts."

Derva looked around the room, checking where the attention of all the other patrons lay. I could have told her, no one was listening. It wasn't that kind of place.

"People have been back to the site. Their investigations

show no trace of explosives or evidence of them in the debris. They've recovered some of the crew," she whispered.

"No evidence? I saw the device. My suit will have a record of its findings, the messages I sent, the readings from the explosion and the battle." I leaned forward, placing one hand on the table and pointing at her with the other. "Get your teams to look there."

"They did. They found nothing. Your suit memory shows nothing from the moment of your arrival at the city and arriving back at Base 1. The first readings they could find are of your approach to Base 1 and surfacing in their moon-pool."

"What? That's not possible." I must have said it a little loud, a customer, a new one, turned to look in my direction. Just a glance on his way to the toilets at the back. He didn't recognise me, but then in the dark bar it was hard to recognise anyone. I knew him. The last time I had seen his face, he was swinging a fist in my direction whilst two of his friends held me still.

"Corin?" Derva prompted me out of the silence.

"Someone must have wiped the memory."

"It might have been damaged it in the battle?" she suggested.

"No, it wasn't. Believe me you know when a Fish-Suit has been damaged, especially if you're wearing it at the time. Someone is covering this up. What about the VIKYN submarines? What about their attack on the city?"

"VIKYN representatives have been in contact about a rogue group who stole some of their vehicles. Apparently, they are having a little trouble with some religious fundamentalists in their company. The worship of something called Thor, a warrior god of some sort, has resurfaced. They have assured us that they are taking all the necessary action to retrieve their submarines and deal with the insurgents."

"Bollocks. Absolute bollocks. Those submarines were

well armed, well crewed, and they knew what they were doing." I shook my head. Someone was playing with me, with the situation. It had all got political when all I wanted was a taste of revenge, and I knew where to get it. "I need to pee."

She sat alone at the table as I made my way to the toilet. The door creaked open, but the fellow stood at the urinal didn't turn round. Eye contact in a man's toilet was something to be avoided. I let the door close, rolled my shoulders, stretched my arms, and let the anger rise. The deaths at the Silent City. Elena's taunt that she knew something about Tyler's death. The death of my child and that of my crew. My hands closed into fists.

"It is good to see you again, and this time with no friends to help you out," I said as the door clicked shut.

He turned, hand still holding on to his cock. All he managed to say was a truncated, "What?"

My first punch hit him square on the jaw, the second on his shoulder, third in gut. After that, I stopped counting.

.

# ACKNOWLEDGMENTS

My thanks to Julia 'Kitvaria' Serene for reading, enjoying, pointing out the errors and telling others about the book.

It means lot when someone tells you they liked the book and recommend it to others.

With that in mind, if you liked the book tell everyone and if you would leave a review or rating on Goodreads and Amazon I would be really grateful.

Thanks

G R Matthews

# ABOUT THE AUTHOR

G R Matthews began reading in the cot. His mother, at her wits end with the constant noise and unceasing activity, would plop him down on the soft mattress with an encyclopedia full of pictures then quietly slip from the room. His father, ever the pragmatist, declared, that they should, "throw the noisy bugger out of the window." Happily, this event never came to pass (or if it did, he bounced well). Growing up, he spent Sunday afternoons on the sofa watching westerns and Bond movies with the self-same parent who had once wished to defenestrate him. When not watching the six-gun heroes or spies being out-acted by their own eyebrows, he devoured books like a hungry wolf in the dead of winter. Beginning with Patrick Moore and Arthur C Clarke he soon moved on to Isaac Asimov. However, one wet afternoon in a book shop in his home town, not far from the standing stones of Avebury, he came across a book by David Eddings - and soon Sci-Fi gave way to Fantasy. Many years later, G R Matthews finally realised a dream and published his own fantasy novel, The Stone Road, in the hopes that other hungry wolves out there would find a hearty meal. You can follow him on twitter @G_R_Matthews or visit his website at www.grmatthews.com

Made in the USA
Charleston, SC
12 September 2016